raven summer

raven summer

DAVID ALMOND

DELACORTE PRESS

All rights reserved. Published in the United States by Delacorte Press, an imprint of Random House Children's Books, a division of Random House, Inc., New York. Originally published in Great Britain as *Jackdaw Summer* by Hodder Children's Books, a division of Hachette Children's Books, London, a Hachette Livre Company, London, in 2008.

Delacorte Press is a registered trademark and the colophon is a trademark of Random House, Inc.

Visit us on the Web! www.randomhouse.com/teens

Educators and librarians, for a variety of teaching tools, visit us at www.randomhouse.com/teachers

Library of Congress Cataloging-in-Publication Data
Almond, David.
[Jackdaw summer]
Raven summer / David Almond.—1st ed.
p. cm.
Summary: Led to an abandoned baby by a raven, fourteen-year-old Liam seems fated to meet two foster children who have experienced the world's violence in very different ways as he struggles to understand war, family problems, and friends who grow apart.
ISBN: 978-0-385-73806-4 (TR)—ISBN: 978-0-385-90715-6 (GLB)—
ISBN: 978-0-375-89385-8 (e-book)
[1. Foundlings—Fiction. 2. Interpersonal relations—Fiction. 3. Conduct of life—Fiction. 4. Fate and fatalism—Fiction. 5. Northumberland (England)—Fiction. 6. England—Fiction.]
I. Title.
PZ7.A448Rav 2009
[Fic]—dc22
2009001661

The text of this book is set in 11.5-point Bauer Bodoni.

Printed in the United States of America

10 9 8 7 6 5 4 3 2

First American Edition

For Jill Hughes

Thanks to Nicola Davies
for her information
about imprinting

one

1

It starts and ends with the knife. I find it in the garden. I'm
with Max Woods. We're messing about, digging for treasure,
like we did when we were little kids. As always there's nothing
but stones and roots and dust and worms. Then there it is, just
below the surface, a knife with a wooden handle in a leather
sheath. I lever it out of the earth. The curved blade's all tar-
nished, the handle's filthy, the sheath's blackened and stiff and
starting to rot away.

I laugh in triumph.

"Treasure at last!"

"Huh!" says Max. "It's just an old pruning knife."

"Course it's not! It's from the ancient Romans or the
reivers. It's a weapon of war!"

I hold it up towards the sun.

"I name thee . . . Death Dealer!" I say.

Max mutters under his breath and rolls his eyes. I stab the knife into the earth to clean. I wipe it on the grass. I spit on it and rub it. I pick up a stone and try to sharpen it.

Then a bird flutters onto the grass six feet away.

"Hello, crow," I say.

"It's a raven, townie," says Max. He imitates its call. "Jak jak! Jak! Jak jak!"

The raven bounces, croaks back at him.

Jak jak! Jak jak!

"It's after the worms," says Max.

"No. It's seen something shiny! It's seen Roman gold! There, look!"

I dig like a maniac for a few daft moments. I stab the earth, plunge the knife deeper. Then my hand slips and blood's pouring out from my wrist. I scream, then laugh at myself and press my finger to the little wound.

Max mutters again.

"Sometimes I think you're crackers," he says.

"Me too," I say.

We lie in the grass and stare at the sky. It's early summer, hardly more than spring, but the sun's been pouring down for weeks. The ground's baked hard, the grass is already getting scorched. It'll be the hottest summer ever, and the story is they'll keep on getting hotter. The dust and soil's like a crust on my hands and arms. It mingles on my wrist with the dark red of drying blood, just like a painting or a map.

A low-flying jet thunders over us, then another, then another.

"Begone, you beasts!" I call.

"Come and have a lie-down, lads!" he shouts. "I'll make sure you're covered up nice and warm!"

Then Max says, "Would you believe it?"

It's the raven again, in the branches of a yew tree above us.

Jak jak! Jak jak!

"Can't be the same one," I say. "Can it?"

"Looks like it," says Max.

It flies ahead, stops, flies ahead, stops. The hiker ahead of us has stopped, too. He's looking back, shielding his eyes with his hand. Hard to make him out at this distance. It could be a woman.

"What do you *want*?" I say to the bird.

Max grins.

"It's definitely been tamed by somebody," he says.

We follow it as it flies on. Up by the Bull, it perches on a wall, dead still, like it's *waiting*.

"Weird," I say.

"Aye. Very weird."

As we stand here, an army lorry rumbles past. There's a bunch of soldiers in the back, hardly older than we are. They grin out at us.

"Join the army, lads!" yells one of them.

"It's a great life!" yells another. "Get good mates! See the world! Learn to maim and kill!"

Then they're gone, off to play war games up at Otterburn, where the camps and the exercise grounds and the firing ranges are.

The bird leads us through the covered lane between two cottages by the pub. It takes long hops in there, lifting its wings, half flying. Its croak echoes off the walls, its wings flap against them. Then we're out into Drogan's Field and heading away from the houses towards Benner's Brook. We stop on the little wooden bridge. The bird's in the copse on the other side, on the path that winds between the birch trees. We can just see the hiker's cap through the trees.

I spit down into the water, and watch the little gobs of phlegm curling away.

Jak jak! Jak jak!

"Shut up!" says Max.

There's another jet, but far off this time. I close my eyes, turn my face to the sun, feel it burning into me. What will the summers be like when we're grown up, when we've got kids of our own? Will families like mine and Max's be battling each other for water, like families round here used to battle for sheep and cows? I imagine struggling with him, fighting with knives to the death beside a well.

Jak! Jak jak!

"Mebbe we should just go back," says Max.

"Aye. This is stupid."

But it feels just as stupid to turn back.

We play Poohsticks, just like we used to: kick twigs off the bridge into the stream, count the seconds till they come through to the other side. I get my knife and scrape our initials into the bridge's wooden rail. There they are, along with fading initials of dozens of kids going back year after year.

Jak jak! Jak jak!

We shrug and go into the copse and beyond it into the next field, where a ram glares at us and the sheep bleat and scatter stupidly away. Then across Castle Lane and to a gate onto the old reivers' track that leads down towards the river. The field drops steeply to the river. It's all uneven and tussocky and there's lengths of barbed wire from an old fence all tangled up with fallen stones from an ancient wall. The castle turrets are just visible higher upriver. Max grabs my arm and holds me back.

"Watch your step," he hisses.

There's an adder basking in the sun. Just a few feet ahead of us, curled up in the grass, rusty red, with the line of black diamonds all along its back.

"Hello, snake," I whisper.

I crouch down and stare. It's so beautiful.

Max stamps, and the adder uncurls. It lifts its head, seems to look straight at us, then slides down between two stones into the earth.

"What a beauty!" I whisper.

Jak jak! Jak jak!

Down here there's a bulge of bare black stone with ancient art carved into it: cup and ring marks, swirls and loops made by unknown people at an unknown time.

Jak jak! Jak jak!

We follow the call. There's an ancient farmhouse, Rook Hall, a small square fortified place with thick walls, windows like arrow slits. Places like this were built in the days of slaughter. An ancient farmer and his family and his beasts took shelter in here when raiders came down from the north. Its doors disappeared an age ago. Its roof's fallen in. Further down, there's the river, then the opposite bank, then moorland and emptiness. The footpath turns down there, follows the river as it curves northwards. The hiker's standing on the bank, staring down into the water. The air by the water trembles in the heat.

11

The raven's perched on the ruined wall of Rook Hall. It's dead silent now. It's all so ancient here: just water and stones and trees and the birds. Fish in the river, snakes in the earth, creatures all around us, watching, hiding, trembling, scared.

We used to talk, Max and I, about what we'd do if the worst things happened, if the awful things out there in the world arrived in Northumberland. We talked about the adventures we'd have, just like little kids do. We'd head northwards with a tent. We'd take weapons and fishing rods and traps. We'd hunt and fish and hide. Maybe we'd find other kids we could team up with. We'd start a new society out here in Northumberland. We'd make a better world, close to nature: no violence, no wars, no waste. A couple of times we even practiced it. We spent whole days walking north on the old trails. We found places that'd be great to hide in, secret sheltered places close to streams, away from public view but with a good view of any strangers or pursuers. We even stashed stuff away in some places: tins of food, compasses, knives, just in case the worst comes to the worst.

Max laughs about all that now. He says how daft we were, how childish, but it's not really that long ago. And I still dream about it. I dream that war has come at last. I'm running and hiding, I'm heading north again, all alone. I'm at one of our hiding places. I'm lifting a great rock to get at the stashed boxes beneath.

Jak! Jak!

The call's louder now, more insistent. The bird flutters down into the ruined hall.

Jak! Jak! Jak! Jak!

We peer into the shadows. The bird furiously flaps its

wings. We both know we're scared and we're scared to admit it.

Max licks his lips.

"Hell's teeth," he says. "It's just a bird!"

I reach for the knife, draw it out. It fits snugly in my hand. We clamber in over the fallen stones and the raven croaks one last time and flies straight into the sky and it's gone.

We can't help laughing. My heart's thudding.

"We're so stupid!" says Max.

"I know!" I say. "It was just a stupid bird!"

"It thought we were *chasing* it!" said Max.

Then we shut up. There's a tiny sound somewhere in Rook Hall.

We can't turn away. We can't run. We pick our way over the rubble and sheep droppings towards the sound of crying. And there it is, on a pile of broken stones. It's a baby, wrapped in a brown blanket, in a basket. There's a scribbled note pinned to the blanket. PLESE LOOK AFTER HER RITE. THIS IS A CHILDE OF GOD. And there's a jam jar filled with notes and coins at her side.

3

We carry her home the long way, through the fields. We climb over gates. We pass the baby carefully across the gates to each other. We walk on the hard rutted ground at the edge of crops of corn and barley.

We take a break in the shade under a hawthorn tree. I stroke the baby's cheek and she catches my finger in her hand and holds it tight. Max says that's what babies always do. He knows about babies. He's got a whole string of sisters and brothers. He leans down till his face is right down in the basket. He sighs and grins.

"Smell her," he says.

"Eh?"

"It's one of the things about them. They smell lovely. Weird, but lovely. Go on."

So I lean right down. The baby touches my face and I feel her tiny sharp fingernails on my cheek. I smell the weird lovely smell of her.

"See?" says Max.

"Aye."

"That's what you once smelt like—till you started turning into a big farty lump."

We hold up the jar of money and peer inside. There's fivers and tenners and coins from now, and there's notes and coins from the last century: big five-pound notes, big pennies and little farthings and shiny sixpences. I unscrew the lid and take out some notes, fold them and stuff them in my pocket. I stare at Max.

"We *can't*," he says.

"Who would know?"

"Somebody. I don't know. Whoever's it is."

"Mebbe it's finders keepers, Max. And we could stash it in one of the hiding places for when we need it."

He shakes his head.

"What a dreamer," he says. "Anyway, it's not like *you* need it, Patrick Lynch's son."

I sigh. He seems so boring these days, like he can't wait to grow up, like he won't do anything reckless anymore. I take the money out of my pocket and hold it out to him.

"*You* take it, then. Go on, be daft for once."

He doesn't, of course.

"Mebbe there'll be a reward," he says. "Mebbe nobody'll claim it and it'll all be ours in the end."

"Aye," I say, "that's sensible."

Another jet booms by. The baby cries again. I stuff a few

notes in my pocket while he looks at her. I put the rest back in the jar.

"She'll be hungry," says Max, so we lift the basket and set off again.

We go through the last field, over the last gate, head for my house.

Dad's window's still open. We put the baby on the kitchen table. There's a yell from upstairs. Max jumps. I grin.

"It's nothing," I say. "He does that when he's stuck. When the story's going nowhere or when one of his characters is causing problems."

"Sounds like he's getting attacked," says Max.

Dad yells again, like he's in agony.

I point to my head.

"It's like he lives in here, not in the real world."

"Weird," says Max. "Where's your mum?"

"She went off to Newcastle this morning."

The baby's still whimpering.

"She'll need milk," says Max. "But what kind?"

I stroke the baby's cheek, and smile at her, then I go upstairs. I stash the money from the jar in my bedroom. I knock at Dad's door.

I hear a grunt, then he calls,

"Who's that?"

"Me."

"I thought you were with Max all day."

"I am."

"No, you're not. You're knocking at my door. Is your mother not back yet?"

"No."

16

"*Tch.* Look, I'm in the *middle* of something."

I want to shove the door open. It's not long since I used to sit under his desk drawing pictures and scribbling as he wrote. Not that long since I even sat on his knee as he wrote.

"We found something," I say through the door.

"Good!"

"We don't know what to do about it."

"Hell's teeth, Liam! You're a big lad now, you know."

He comes to the door. There he is with his scruffy beard and his hair all messy. There's the screen glaring on the desk behind him. There's the pages of scribble lying all over the floor. There's the walls filled with books and books and books.

"I'm in the *middle* of something," he says again.

He yells at the sky and shakes his fists as a jet flies past.

"Go and bomb Tony Blair!"

"We found a baby," I say.

"You found a *what*?"

"A baby, by the river."

He stares at me, like I'm a hundred miles away.

"And where's the baby now?" he says.

"Downstairs, on the kitchen table. And she needs some milk."

4

Even when he's standing there looking at her and touching her cheek with his finger, he says,

"You're having me on, aren't you? It's one of your lot, Max, isn't it?" He rolls his eyes. "And how come you just happened to be at the right spot to find her?"

"A raven took us," I say.

"It led us through the village and down the fields," says Max.

Dad grins.

"Hey, nice touch, lads. But you'll have to write it yourself if you want all this in a story. I've not got the time."

He raises his hands.

"Look, Liam," he says. "I know it's a pain that I'm so busy, but I've got to get on with this book."

"And there was this as well," I say.

I put the jar of money and the note onto the table.

He narrows his eyes.

"Is this true?" He sighs. "It is, isn't it? That's all I need."

Dad calls the police. Max holds his knuckle to the baby's mouth and lets her suck on it.

"She thinks it'll give her milk," he says. "She'll be bawling when she sees there's no chance." He strokes her cheek. "There, there. We're going to sort you out, sweetheart."

Dad puts the phone down. The police are on their way. He stares at the baby. She opens her mouth and screams.

"What should we do, Max?" asks Dad.

Max looks inside the blanket.

"She needs her nappy changed," he says.

"We can't do that," says Dad. "We should wait for the police before we go ahead and do anything like that."

The baby bawls on. Dad makes a coffee. He scribbles in a notebook.

"So it wasn't a crow or a rook?" he says. "They all look the same to me. Birds. Black."

"Raven," says Max. "It's bigger than a crow."

"And it was the same one, all the way?"

"Aye," says Max.

Dad scribbles.

"You can tame them, can't you?" he says.

"Aye. And eat them if you're daft enough."

Dad nibbles his thumbnail. He scratches his beard. He peers into the jar and scribbles again.

"And there was a hiker, with a red hat?"

"Yes," I say. "Like there's always hikers."

"And the snake was an adder, yes? And it's the heat they like, yes?"

"Aye," says Max.

"And did you ever hear about anything like this happening out here before, Max?"

"Happens all the time," says Max. "We're always finding babies by the river with jars of loot beside them."

I stash the knife with the money in my bedroom before the police arrive. There's two of them, PC Ball ands WPC Jenkins. They're wearing bulletproof vests over their short-sleeved shirts.

"Do you really need to turn up like we're a bunch of crack dealers?" says Dad.

"It's policy, Mr. Lynch," says PC Ball. "No need to take it personally."

"You never know who's got a gun or a knife in their pocket," says WPC Jenkins.

"Even out here in the peaceful spots," says Ball.

He looks at me: I look straight back at him. He grins.

"Or are you all little angels out here, eh?" He winks. "Any chance of a cuppa, sir?"

They write it all down: the journey, the discovery, the journey home. They write about the snake. They raise their eyebrows at the bit about the raven, but they write it anyway. They write a description of the hiker.

"Walking gear," says PC Ball. "Red cap. Could be a man or a woman. Not too specific, is it, lads?"

"They weren't close by," I say. "And the sun was glaring."

"And Rook Hall?" he says. "It's on a walking route, eh? So they left her in a place where they knew she'd be found."

"*They?*" says Dad.

"It's usually the mum," says PC Ball. "They're too young, they can't cope, something like that."

"She'll need help as much as the baby," says WPC Jenkins. "She'll turn up in the end. She'll not be able to stay away from her child."

They phone headquarters: the area around Rook Hall needs to be sectioned off and searched.

"They'll be contacting all the hospitals now," says WPC Jenkins. "They'll get messages to the GPs. Somebody somewhere'll know something. They're looking for the hiker. These things don't stay mysteries for long."

A motorbike screams on the military road. A jet howls past. Dad growls at it. PC Ball sips his tea.

"Peaceful out here, isn't it?" he says.

An ambulance turns up. A couple of young paramedics in orange jumpsuits come in.

"Abandoned?" says the girl, Doreen. She lifts the baby. "Who'd abandon a lovely little lass like this?"

She holds the baby up high.

"Girls are *gorgeous*!" she says. "But my goodness, they can stink! *Pooee!* But guess what I brought, just for you? Nappies! Hurray!"

She changes the baby on the draining board. She murmurs all the time, she makes her eyes wide and bright, she coos and squeaks.

"Perfect as a picture. And sweetly smelling as a rose. Now, would our lovely little girly like some *milk?*"

She feeds it from a bottle. The baby snuffles and sucks, and after a while just goes to sleep, and Doreen sits there with the baby on her lap. She smiles and sighs.

"You found a proper little angel, lads," she says.

The paramedics take the baby away. The police take the basket and the note and the jar of cash. They say they'll be in touch. There'll be lots more to ask, lots more to talk about. They're just about to leave when PC Ball says, like he's suddenly remembered to say it,

"Thank you, lads. You've been good citizens."

"What else could we do?" says Max.

"Oh, you'd be surprised." He tightens the straps on his bulletproof vest. "Some lads in your position, seeing all that cash . . ." He grins at me. "Know what I mean, lads?"

I look straight back at him.

"No," I say.

"That's great. And you weren't—even a good lad like you, Liam, even for a few seconds—tempted, were you?"

"What?" snaps Dad. "What *exactly* are you suggesting?"

"Oh, nothing, sir," says PC Ball. "But in our position, you always have to allow yourself to wonder."

And he looks at me for a moment, then they're gone.

We sit at the kitchen table. Dad says he should get on, but he doesn't move. Scribbles a bit in his notebook. Stares and ponders. He's doing what he does to just about everything, turning it into a story.

"How old do you think she was?" he says.

"A few months," says Max. "Mebbe four."

I imagine Mum holding me up high when I was a few months old and saying, Boys are *gorgeous*! We were in Newcastle way back then, stony broke. We were right on the brink, Mum used to say.

Dad keeps on scribbling.

The fields are shimmering outside the kitchen window. There's cattle, sheep, hedges, copses, the blue blue sky. And more jets, black and silent over the hazy wind turbines at Hallington Ridge.

Then there's footsteps outside, and here's Gordon Nattrass at the door. I go to him.

"You said you'd come to the field," he says. "And you didn't."

"We got sidetracked," I tell him.

"You weren't avoiding us, then?"

"Course we weren't."

We watch each other.

He's still carrying the saw. There's a sack slung over his shoulder. "You're missing out, brother," he says. "We had a great time." Then he goes. A few drops of blood drip from the sack as he walks away.

5

It's late when Mum comes home. Max has gone. Dad's upstairs. There's a smell of cigarette smoke on her, and that look in her eyes she has these days when she comes back from town.

"What a day," she says. "Lunch with Sue, then of course the gallery launch, then of course we go on for drinks."

"But you drove," I say.

"I just had a teeny weeny bit." She pours a big glass of red wine. She points to the ceiling. "His nibs is at work?"

I nod.

She puts her hands to her face and beams.

"They're going to show *my* work, Liam. In a brand-new gallery right slap bang in the middle of Newcastle. This is *big*, son."

She swigs her wine, closes her eyes, sighs.

"It's not an angle, Mr. Lynch. And after all, there's plenty magic at work in your stories."

"But they are *stories*."

"Exactly," he says. "They are stories, and this is—"

"The real world," says Dad.

"Correct," says Joe. "But as you've said many times yourself, the real world is the very very strangest of places."

Dad snorts again.

"Of course it is!" he says. "But it doesn't need magic to make it strange."

Joe just smiles.

"There'll be a perfectly rational explanation," says Dad.

"Could be," says Joe. He rubs his hands and grins again. "But until the explanation turns up, what other approach do you suggest we take?"

Six o'clock that evening we're all in front of the TV. Mum's got a glass of wine. Dad's got a pint of beer. I'm drinking Coke.

"I warn you," says Dad. "They'll miss out most of what you said. They always do. They never get it right. Don't be surprised if you're not even on at all, specially if there's been another knifing in Middlesbrough, or some little kid's been mauled by a dog in Wallsend."

He swigs his beer and grunts.

Mum's all grins.

"Liam and Max on the telly!" she says. She squeezes my arm and giggles. "Hey, we should have put some of my paintings up in the background, Liam! Make sure we do it next time!"

Dad grunts again.

"Next time!" he says.

Then he shuts up. We're the first item on the news. It starts with stuff about the baby and appeals for information. They ask the hiker in the red cap to come forward. A doctor says he knows the mother'll be in great distress, but she will of course be treated with great compassion. So please come forward. Then it slips into Mysterious Events in Secret Northumberland. There's a swirl of mist, the cry of a raven, a flash of black wings, a casket of treasure, then a film of Rook Hall and the police searching around it.

"Here we are in the twenty-first century," drones Joe Tynan, "but could ancient forces—forces of magic and mystery—still be at work?" He reads the message in a stagey voice. "Please look after her right," he says. "This is a child of God." He widens his eyes. "What could it all mean?" he whispers.

"It means zilch!" says Dad. He glares at the screen. "You could say that about every single kid that's ever been born."

Then there's Max looking bright-eyed and smart and me dead scruffy as we tell the tale. "And the raven really did lead you?" is Joe's final question.

"Aye," says Max. "It came into Liam's garden and led us away."

Then there's a few of Dad's books with mist swirling again, and an adder slithering across them. Then Dad himself, an interview from ages back, from when his books were just starting to sell. He looks really young and fit and bright. "Yes," he says, "truth and fiction merge into each other. We try to keep them apart, but how can we? We live

30

in a miraculous world, a world that is filled with the most amazing possibilities."

Dad grunts and groans and grinds his teeth.

"Hell's teeth!" he says.

He flings a cushion at the TV and he sinks his beer fast.

7

We do get on national TV, a little item at the end of the ten o'clock news. We're in the News of the World next to a report about Michael Jackson's nose cracking up. The *Sunday Times* links our story to a travel feature about the beauties of Northumbria.

The attention lasts a week or so, but pretty soon it all starts dying off. Dad's right, and other stories start taking over. There's a big drugs raid in Middlesbrough. A couple of Newcastle United players kick each other half to death on the quayside. Thirty asylum seekers jump ship in Blyth. Then the big one: a journalist called Greg Armstrong who grew up in Hexham has been taken hostage in Baghdad. A couple of groups claim to have him. His wife and kids are on TV, pleading for his release. He can't be traced.

The police visit farms and cottages for miles around. No answers about the baby. No information. The red-capped hiker's never found. A new story turns up during the search: the death of Thomas Fell. His body's found in an ancient cottage in a valley below Cheviot. Must have been there months. It's almost eaten away to bone. He must have been eighty years old. He was a prisoner of war in World War II who never went home again. He became a wanderer, a tramp, living alone in the northern moors. He lived out in the open in summer, in abandoned cottages when the cold came. He was often seen roaming, dreaming. He was rumored to be a good man, a kind man. But he was silent and elusive, a man who loved his solitude. Not a man for making friends or having family. Kept himself to himself, never lost his thick Bavarian accent. Left behind a sheaf of poems in German, a box full of treasures dug out from the earth: arrowheads, coins, stone knives from right back in the Stone Age. The story's told, then fades away, like all the stories in the news.

8

The days heat up. There's restrictions on water use. The brook slows to a trickle. The river sinks. Max and I play football in the garden, climb trees, wander through the lanes. We camp out every night in the garden in the breathless nights. I polish the knife, I sharpen it, I soften its sheath. I dream about it resting snug in my hand. We talk about the baby. I spin yarns about her: she's a fairy baby and the money's fairy gold; she's come through some kind of time warp from the time of the border raids; she's the child of some barmy farmer and a witch.

We play with the kids on the field beside the school. The kids keep on laughing at us for how stupid we looked on telly, but they want to know the story again and again. Did you really not nick some of the money? they say. You must be stupid, they say.

One day Gordon Nattrass gets on about Greg Armstrong.

"Me dad was at school with him," he says. "Says he was a right snobby ponce. He was probably poking and prying where he shouldn't've been. We're not weeping no tears for him. What was he doing there anyway?"

"What do you mean, What was he doing there?" I say.

"I mean what I say, brother. What's Iraq got to do with him? Why couldn't he stay where he come from, in Northumberland?"

"Like the Nattrasses have done?" I say.

He pauses. He looks me in the eye.

"Aye, Liam, like the Nattrasses have always done. Mebbe it'd be better if we all stayed where we come from. It'd save a lot of bother."

He laughs.

"I'm keeping an eye on the Net. Mebbe it won't be long till we see the video of him getting his head sliced off."

He grins at me.

"Aye," he says. "I know what you think. I'm a throwback. I'm like something from the Dark Ages. And guess what, brother? I couldn't give a toss."

We play endless war games. I throw myself into it and I get wilder and wilder. I'm growing, getting stronger. I let my hair grow long. Sometimes I go out with Death Dealer resting at my hip. We rip branches off the trees. We make bows and arrows and catapults and spears. We strip our tops off in the baking heat and we battle and fight and charge. The low-flying jets roar over us. We don't cover our ears. We yell curses at them. We yell, "Bomb them right back to the Stone Age!" We stripe face paint and dye on our skin. Nobody gets really hurt, but all our bodies get nicked and scratched and bruised. Sometimes I see Max standing back from it all, watching me as if I'm a million miles away. He's suddenly friendly with a girl called Kim Shields. They've started spending time at each other's houses. They go walking together. I feel far away from him. Sometimes I feel far away from everything, like I'm spinning away into outer space.

Sometimes in the middle of the wild games on the field I find myself at the school windows. I look in at the classrooms I sat in when I first came here: the small desks and chairs, the paintings on the walls, the illustrated books. I remember the smells of our bodies on warm afternoons, the songs we sang, the plays we acted, the delicious lunches, the sweet teachers. I go to high school in Hexham now, and it's fine, but it's great to press my face to the window and look into the past, to see me and Max and the other little ones painting together, to see Nattrass scowling in the corner where he's been put until his temper calms down.

One day I find Max standing beside me, looking into the classroom with me. Kim's a few yards behind, like he's just left her and she's waiting for him to go back to her.

"It was easy, wasn't it?" I say.

"What was?"

"Being little. Being looked after all the time."

He shrugs.

"Suppose so. Why? Do you want to be like that again?"

"Dunno."

I raise my hand. There's a homemade spear in it. I pretend I'm going to plunge it into him, then I howl and run back fast into the field.

I don't want to be little again. But at the same time I do. I want to be me like I was then, and me as I am now, and me like I'll be in the future. I want to be me and nothing but me. I want to be crazy as the moon, wild as the wind, and still as the earth. I want to be every single thing it's possible to be. I'm growing and I don't know how to grow. I'm living but I haven't started living yet. Sometimes I simply disappear from myself. Sometimes it's like I'm not here in the world at all and I simply don't exist. Sometimes I can hardly think. My head just drifts, and the visions that come seem so vivid. Max still comes to the tent sometimes, but we're getting more impatient with each other.

One night he's talking about Kim and he says,

"You should find a girl yourself."

"I don't want a girl."

"You should."

He even says,

"And you should cut your hair, or at least keep it cleaner."

"What?"

"That's what they like, Liam."

"What? How old are you, forty-seven?"

"No," he says. "But I *am* growing up."

He lies there. He looks at me. Probably we're both thinking we don't want to argue. We've been good mates. We've done so many things together. So we say nothing for a while. Then he starts talking again, and he starts like he'd have started in the old days, like he'd thought something really important about hiding places or treasure or how to trap rabbits.

"I've been thinking lots of things," he starts. "And talking to my dad and the teachers."

"Aye?"

"Aye. About the future. About the directions I should take."

"Aye?"

"Aye. It's obvious, really. I should be something like an agricultural engineer."

"What?"

"Aye. My dad deals with them all the time. Says there's great opportunities."

I let him go on about what the job is, what it can lead to. We go to sleep soon afterwards.

I think of him dreaming of being married to Kim and of tractors and harvesters and conferences in nice country hotels while my dreams are filled with war, with snakes, with bloody wounds, disaster and death. I keep feeling blood trickling over my skin.

9

One day Mum's spreading cream onto a bruise on my chest.
She's inspecting all the nicks and scabs and cuts. She tells me I
should take more care, but Dad just snorts at her.

"He's just being a proper lad," he says. "Let him be.
What's the point of living in the backwoods if you can't get a
bit of blood on you?"

Then he points at my body, at all the stripes and nicks and
bruises on it.

"Anyway, look," he says. "His skin's just like one of your
paintings."

She pauses in her movements for a moment. She regards
me, then begins to touch the colors and marks more gently
with her fingertips.

"Well, well," she murmurs as I back away.

She makes a rectangle with her index fingers and thumbs and looks at my skin through it.

"You're right," she says. "The boy's a living work of art."

10

One Saturday morning I'm wandering alone when my name's called out. There's laughter. I look around stupidly. A stone falls from the sky, then another. Then Nattrass and a couple of his mates, Eddie and Ned, are coming out from behind a dilapidated cow shed.

"You're looking dozy, brother," says Nattrass. "What's up? You in love or something?"

His mates laugh along with him. They're all filthy, streaked with earth and sweat.

"We saw you," he says, "and we thought, We could probably let him in on it. He'll have the guts for it."

"For what?" I say.

"Come and see." He smiles. "If you let on, mind, you'll suffer for it."

They lead me back to where they came from. Past the cow-shed, into the long narrow allotment behind Nattrass's house. It's all overgrown. A broken greenhouse with an ash tree growing in it. Brambles and raspberries growing wild. It's Nattrass's place, his hangout, his hideout. I remember it well. Used to play here so often, until we started growing apart, until I started hanging out with Max.

They've cleared a space. They've marked out a square. They're digging a pit. Their spades are resting on the great pile of earth that's been dug out.

"Go on, then," says Nattrass. "Ask what we're up to."

He wipes the sweat from his brow with a filthy hand.

I look down into the pit. No treasure, as usual: just stones and tangled roots and soil. It's maybe six feet wide. It's already two feet deep.

"Go on," he says.

"OK, so what you doing?" I ask.

"We're digging your grave, Liam! Hahahaha!"

His mates roar with laughter along with him.

"Just joking," he says. "Get a spade, Liam, come and help, otherwise come back and have a look tomorrow."

"If you've got the nerve for it," says Eddie.

"Aye, if you've got the nerve," says Ned.

They grunt and laugh together. I spit.

"Just one thing," says Nattrass. "We don't want you telling nobody. OK, brother?"

I just look at him and turn away.

I go back the next day. As I walk by the cowshed, I hear kids' voices. Two girls are coming towards me, leaving the allotment.

"Don't go, Liam," says one of them, Nancy Sloane. "It's horrible. It's cruel."

But it just entices me. I shrug and smile and step past them.

There's a little cluster of kids there.

"Let Liam through," says Nattrass.

I sidle through. I look down with the others. The pit's three feet deep now. There are three adders in it, two of them curled up dead still, the other slithering, squirming. It tries to raise its head towards the pit edge but it could never reach. Nattrass laughs and knocks it back with a stick. There's a couple of mice in there as well, hunched together in a corner, petrified.

"They're savage little buggers, Liam," he says. "Mebbe they're magic to townies like you, but they bite farmers. They bite dogs. They bite ramblers. They bite little bairns playing in the fields. And they're ten times worse in hot years like this. So I been out catching them. Better that they're here in my pit than out there being wild and doing harm."

He pokes the squirming snake again. It bares its fangs. Nattrass licks his lips and spits.

"See what I mean, brother?" he said. "It'd bite you as soon as look at you."

I pick up a fallen twig from the grass. I touch one of the snakes. It squirms, turns, bares its fangs. I touch it again. It bites. I feel the vibrations through the twig.

Nattrass grins.

"That's right, Liam," he says. "Get them angry."

He looks around the faces.

"So," he says, "who's going first?"

43

He's got a plank, six inches wide. He drops it across the middle of the pit.

There's laughter, intakes of breath, muttered curses. A couple of kids head off home straightaway.

"Aye. Shove off if you like," says Nattrass. "But remember, not a word. Otherwise . . ." He laughs. "Chickens!"

"I'll do it," says Eddie.

"I know *you* would," says Nattrass. "But what about you, Liam, eh?" His eyes widen as he approaches. I clench my fists, get ready for him. But he just punches me gently in the ribs.

"Just joking, man. I wouldn't ask nobody to do something I wouldn't do myself."

He steps onto the plank and walks straight across without a care in the world. He does it again. Stands in the middle and bounces. Pretends he's falling, then steps across the three-foot gap from the plank to safety. We all do it. It's easy. We shudder and gasp and we're scared we'll fall, but it's easy. We pause. We watch as the squirming snake suddenly opens its jaws and stabs at one of the mice. The mouse shudders, wriggles, lies panting for a few moments, then it's still. The other mouse squeaks, squeaks, squeaks. The snake bites that one, too, and it shudders on the earth and is still. Nattrass sighs, laughs. Another snake starts to move. The two snakes raise their heads six inches from the earth. We crouch at the rim of the pit and watch.

"Go on, my beauties!" murmurs Nattrass. "Go on!"

The snakes eye each other, then dart for each other. They writhe together, then separate and lie at opposite ends of the pit. The third snake moves, slithers around the pit.

We all watch, mesmerized.

"Time for episode two," says Nattrass. "Too easy, that time. Wasn't it?"

He holds up a black scarf.

"This'll add a bit of spice," he says.

He starts wrapping the scarf over his eyes. A few more kids head off home. Again, he does it first. Steps onto the plank, feels his way forward. All the snakes start slithering below him. He moves slowly. Short step, then balance, then short step again. He reaches the other side, pulls the scarf away, makes a fist, grins.

He dangles the scarf in the air.

"Next?"

Eddie does it, then another lad, Rod Hughes, then Ned. Then me. The blackness and the image of the snakes beneath are awful and the crossing is dreadful, terrifying. But it's still easy. You just concentrate: one foot in front of the other, arms out wide, balance, next foot. The worst bit's in the middle where the plank sags under your weight and you feel the snakes' fangs are inches away. But you know you can easily jump to the side, even with the mask on. And the others guide you: *Two more feet, one more foot.* And they hold out their arms if you show any sign of tottering. You know that somebody will reach out, will give you an arm or a hand.

Then it starts to be a joke: *It nearly got you! Aaaaagh, look out! A bit to the left! Oh no, I meant the right! The plank's cracking! Jump! Jump!*

Then prodding, and poking, and shoving. And we're all giggling and laughing and cursing, filled with excitement and terror. And when the mask's on you know that there's nobody there to help, there's only things to make it worse, to make it harder. And you think of the snakes and their slithering shapes and their jaws and fangs and venom. But you do it anyway because it's so weird, it's so engulfing, because you've never done anything like it before. And then of course one of us falls, Eddie Marks, a skinny lad, twelve years old. He topples as we're prodding him. He can't react in time and leap for the rim. He sprawls in the pit. We haul him out even as he's falling. The snakes don't get him. We throw him into the grass and he lies there screaming like a baby and he just won't stop. And most of us are gasping air and shuddering and shaking and stamping and cupping our hands to our mouths and trying not to howl. And Nattrass moves among us, grinning. Then I crack. I go for him. I shove him over and grab him by the throat. He pushes me off and we writhe and struggle on the grass. I try to drag him to the edge of the pit. I see Eddie and Ned coming to us. Any second now there'll be a boot in my face. But it doesn't come, and anyway Nattrass is stronger. He's fighting me off easily. He's laughing.

"Oh, Liam," he says. "I thought folk like you were all peace and love and joy. But you're a bad bugger just like me, aren't you, brother?"

And it's him who's dragging me, and he's laughing and snarling and spitting and bleeding and I'm wishing I had Death Dealer with me to scare him off with.

He gets me to the pit.

"Come and get the bastard!" he yells at the snakes. "Come on!"

The snakes slide and slither but come no nearer.

"Come on!" he yells.

Then there's a man's voice, from Nattrass's house, far away at the end of the overgrown allotment.

"Gordon!"

Nattrass is suddenly dead still.

"Gordon!" comes the voice again.

"Aye, Da?" yells Nattrass.

"What the hell you up to out there?"

Nattrass looks up at me. His dad's disabled, lost his right arm in a tractor accident years ago. He hardly ever gets out. He's hardly ever seen. I remember him, slouched in a dark room on a sofa watching TV. I remember the half-closed door, the smell of piss, stale beer, cigarettes.

"Nowt, Da!" yells Nattrass. "We're just messing about, Da!"

He lets me struggle free.

"That's right, isn't it?" he whispers. "Just messing about. Just playing, eh? Just joking?"

I kneel, stand. There's blood and saliva and snot all over me and I can't tell which is his and which is mine. Nattrass is trying to pull himself together.

"Who'd've thought that Liam Lynch had that in him?" he whispers. He slips closer to me. "You're just like me at heart, Liam. Just like you always were, if truth be told."

"Gordon!" comes the voice again.

"Aye, Da! Aye!"

He waves the others away.

"Shove off," he says. "Shove off, all of you. Quick!"

They start to go.

I spit blood onto the grass.

"We're blood brothers," he says. "Remember? We're linked in blood."

"Piss off, Nattrass," I whisper.

"OK, brother. But you've started something. You know that, don't you?"

"Gordon!"

He grins as I shove past him. I follow the others, past the dilapidated cowshed, heading homeward. Eddie Marks crouches in the next field, vomiting. I whisper to him that he'll be all right, that he'll get over it.

I look back. Nattrass is at the pit's edge. He raises his spade high, plunges it downwards again and again and again, then heads towards the house.

11

The baby's been in hospital for tests. She's being fostered in Newcastle. She's fine and strong and healthy. There's a picture of her with laughing nurses in the *Chronicle*. There's a film of her with her foster parents on ITV.

They've called her Alison.

"It should be Perdita," Dad says. "Like in Shakespeare. *The Winter's Tale*. Perdita, that's the name for foundlings."

I watch Alison on her foster mother's lap. I can still feel her, can still smell her.

"Oh, just look at her," says Mum. "Who could abandon a mite like that?"

"Who *is* she?" I say.

The news moves on to a hit-and-run in Throckley, then

forward to Baghdad. More soldiers have died, including two lads from Gateshead.

"Who is she?" says Mum. "She's a shining light in a dark dark world. That's what she is."

Mum says we should visit her.

"No," says Dad. "Leave her alone to live her own life."

"Live her own life!" says Mam. "She's just a few months old. Anyway, you could say Liam's like one of her family." She laughs. "He's like her big brother."

Dad heads back upstairs. Mum phones social services. Impossible, they say. Then she says she's the mother of Liam Lynch, one of the lads that found her, and they say OK.

So it's into Newcastle the next day, all three of us. Out of the emptiness of the country to the bustle of town. The road in from the west is lined with shops selling saris and fruits and spices. Indian restaurants, Persian restaurants, Turkish takeaways. Dad says how great it is to see. A bit of cultural ferment, he says. Not like the paleface countryside we inhabit.

"So let's move back, then," says Mum. "Be fine with me."

"Course it would, with your galleries and your cafes and your Jack Scott crowds. But d'you think I've got time to move, with my publishing schedule?"

Mum shakes her head and sighs at me.

"And to think he used to tell me he wrote because he loves it," she says.

The foster home is a big double-fronted terraced house with a bright red door and checky curtains at all the windows.

The man that opens the door's wearing a butcher's apron. He holds his hand out. His hand's fat and soft, just like the rest of him. His eyes are tiny and shining.

"You'll be the Lynches," he says. "And you'll be Liam, that found our lovely Alison for us. I'm Phil. And this is Phil as well."

There's a woman just behind him.

"I'm Philomena," she says. "He's Philip. Phil and Phil. Come on in."

We sit on a bench at a massive kitchen table. Two great loaves of bread in the center and a bowl of salad and a big pot of jam. Philip's frying sausages and tomatoes. There's a door into another room half open. A couple of girls sitting in there close together on a sofa. Somebody's playing a guitar. Somebody's banging drums.

Philomena makes coffee for Mum and Dad. She gives me orange juice and a chunk of chocolate cake.

"The baby's snoozing," she says. "We'll get her soon."

She touches my head.

"You looked nice on telly," she says.

"Very whatdeyecallit," says Philip.

"Photogenic," says Philomena.

"That's right," says Philip. He holds up a sizzling sausage with a pair of tongs.

"Oliver!" he calls. "Come and set the table, son! And Crystal, see if the baby's awake, love!"

Oliver's black. He lays down knives and forks and mugs. There's a long-healed deep scar on his cheek, like a knife scar, and another at his throat.

"This is Oliver," says Philip. "He's from Liberia. We're very proud of him."

Philip goes to his side, puts his arm around him.

"Another foundling," says Philip. "Walked away from hell,

spent a year in the backs of trucks all across Europe, then a boat and another boat till he turns up shivering and petrified at the side of Cramlington ring road. What a place to end up, eh? He's strong, he's brave, he's got brains. He's a good boy. Aren't you, son?"

"Aye," says Oliver.

Philip looks at me.

"We don't know we're born, do we?" he says. "We don't know how lucky we are."

I look at Oliver's knife scar, at his calm eyes. He looks straight back at me and smiles.

"They want to send me back," he says.

"To Liberia?"

"Yes, to Liberia."

"They say he's telling lies," says Philomena. "They say he's at least seventeen, but he's only fourteen. They say that the story he's told about his past is not true. But it is true."

"And look at him," says Philip. "Is there a better advert for the whatdeyecallit of the human heart?"

"Resilience," says Philomena.

"Aye, resilience." says Philip. "Hey, maybe you could send your story to Mr. Lynch, Oliver."

"His story?" says Dad.

"It's a tale you wouldn't wish on your worst enemy, and he's writing it. Aren't you, Oliver?"

"Aye," says Oliver.

"Yes," says Dad. "You could, Oliver."

Does he mean it? It happens all the time. People tell him, I've got a story, I've started a novel, do you give advice to hopefuls? He gives slithery replies. Afterwards he shakes his head. Advice? It's simple. Get your backside on a seat, work hard and write.

This time, though, he does look like he's interested. But Oliver shakes his head.

"No," he says. "It is only for me for now. And maybe for those who have loved me." He goes on laying the table. "It takes time to tell the truth, Mr. Lynch."

"You're right," replies Dad. "And even longer to tell it well."

"I know that, Mr. Lynch," says Oliver.

"Here she is!" says Philomena.

12

A skinny girl with wild bleached hair carries the baby in. She's fourteen or so. She sits down close beside me. Puts the baby on my lap.

"It's Liam!" she says. "Look. He's come back for you!"

The baby grips my finger. I lean down to smell her lovely weird scent—I can't help myself. I widen my eyes. I coo and sigh. I smile and smile.

"Hello again," I whisper, then Mum lifts her away and starts her own sighing, smiling, cooing.

"You saved the baby," says the bleach-haired girl. "You're a hero."

Tiny silver studs in her eyebrows. A tiny ring in her nose. A yellow T-shirt, striped tights, and walking boots.

"I'm Crystal," she says. "I'm trouble."

"She's Crystal," says Philomena. "She's lovely."

Crystal smiles.

"Charmer!"

More kids come in, half a dozen of them. They sit and eat their sausages and tomatoes and salad and bread. They're all kinds, all colors, young kids and teenagers. They say hello. They wave at the baby and make big eyes at her. A couple of them ask Dad for autographs.

"That place where you live," says Crystal. "It's beautiful, isn't it?"

I shrug.

"Suppose so," I say.

"Suppose? I seen it on the telly and it *is*." She looks around the table. "It *is*, isn't it? We all seen it on the telly, didn't we? And it is, *isn't* it?" They all laugh. They all agree. "See?" says Crystal. "Don't take it for granted."

She eats her sausages.

"Mebbe I'll come and see you there," she says. "Mebbe I'll come one day with my friend Oliver. That'd get your neighbors talking. Wackos like us two walking through your fields. What d'you think, Ol?"

Oliver looks across the table. He smiles. Crystal winks.

"Better than going back to Liberia, eh?" she says.

She looks at me. A layer of unblemished pale makeup on her skin. Clear green eyes that look right into me.

"Or would you turn us away?" she asks.

I shake my head.

"No," she says. "I think you would not."

We all eat. Mum dances the baby on her lap. She talks with Philomena about sleep and milk and baby clothes.

Crystal's close against me.

"They died," she says.

"*Crys*tal," says Philomena.

"It's OK," says Crystal. "He's a big lad."

She puts a forkful of food into her mouth.

"Who did?" I ask her.

"All of them. Me mam. Me dad. Me sister. It was a house fire." She looks at me again, clear green piercing eyes. "There's no answer to that, is there?"

She's right. No answer.

"I was tiny. Tiny as that little angel there. So I remember nowt."

She tugs up the sleeve of her T-shirt. There's a tattoo of a fire and a bird there.

"There I am," she says.

She grins as I try to work it out.

"The phoenix!" she says. "I'm the bird that rose up from the flames!"

She jumps up and flaps her arms and laughs.

"Look out for the fire!" she calls, then flops down into Philomena's lap. She sits there like a little child, resting against Philomena, watching me. Philomena strokes her head.

Mum continues to hold the baby. She lifts her up before her face.

"What'll happen to this lovely one?" she says.

"Depends," says Philomena. "If there's no leads, no solution to the mystery, in the end she'll go up for adoption."

She touches Alison's cheek.

"And you won't be short of takers," she says. "Will you, my sweet?"

We stand up to leave soon afterwards. Dad's at the door, impatient to get away. Mum whispers with Philomena. Crystal comes to my side.

"I'm not as daft as I seem," she says.

"You're not daft."

"Sometimes I don't know how to be, not with normal folk. Are you normal?"

"I don't know."

"Maybe we're all normal, and maybe we're all daft, all at the same time. What do you think, Liam?"

"Don't know," I say again.

"Me neither." She scratches her head. She presses her index finger to her cheek. The makeup cracks around her fingertip, just like plaster.

"It's all a mystery to me," she says.

I look back as we leave. Oliver's eyes are on me. So are the baby's. So are Crystal's.

"See you," she says.

"See you," I say.

13

"No!" says Dad as we drive towards the empty land to the
west. *"No!* I do not want the responsibility. I do not have the
time. I do not want a mystery child living in our house."

Mum's dead calm.

"Liam and I would look after her," she says. She turns and
winks at me. "Won't we, son?"

"How do you know what you'd be letting yourself in for?"
says Dad. "What about when they come back for her? How
would you cope with letting her go?"

"When they come back for her!" says Mum. "It's not one
of your silly books, you know."

"Silly!" snaps Dad.

The speedo needle swings past ninety.

"Anyway," he says, "it's the last thing *you* need, with your

"And the baby?" she says.

"Don't worry, I won't let them send a single one of them to anybody I haven't been and vetted myself."

Mum chews her lip. Dad's printer whirrs away upstairs. I squeeze her hand.

"Go on," I whisper.

"Philomena," says Mum, "how do I go about becoming a foster carer?"

Philomena laughs.

"Now, why am I not surprised to hear that?" she says. "Well, there's forms to fill in and people to impress, but in the end, it all comes back to the ability to love. And of course Philomena's reference will be very influential." She pauses. We can hear the smiling in her voice. "Would you like me to sort out some application forms for you, Mrs. Lynch?"

That night I'm in the tent with Max. The night's warm and still and the tent door's open. Bats are flickering against the sky. I've told him about Oliver and the war in Liberia and I've been going on about Iraq and Greg Armstrong and beheadings and suicide bombers and all the wars and savagery all around the world and the more I think about it, the worse it all seems, and I tell him how terrible it all is and how it feels like it's all getting closer and it even feels like the start of World War III.

"World War Three!" he mocks.

"Aye. World War Three. I mean, I've just met a lad that's been in a war a million miles away, but there he is right beside us in Newcastle. How much closer *can* you get?"

He shakes his head.

"Hell's teeth," he says. "Listen, I was talking to Kim to-day . . ."

"Oh, aye?"

"Aye. And she was talking about Becky Smith, that lass from Wark. And she reckons—"

"Becky *Smith*," I say.

"Aye. And—"

"There is one thing coming closer," I say.

"What's that?"

"The baby," I say. "I think she might be coming to live with us."

And she does. Mum fills in the forms. She goes to see people at the town hall. They come to visit us. They interview us all. Dad calms down about it. He says yes, of course he'll be happy about having the baby here. Yes, of course he'll love her and look after her. It takes weeks, but all the time they're talking to us and assessing us, we can see they think it's all just marvelous, that Alison's coming to a little bit of paradise.

Philomena visits several times.

"What a perfect place for a her," she says. "What perfect people for her to live with."

And the weeks pass, and the days get even hotter, and the foundling, Alison, is brought to live with us. She sleeps in a cradle in the room just next to mine. The first night, we stand at the cradleside as she sleeps. Her eyes are shifting beneath their lids.

"Who *are* you?" I whisper. "Where did you *come* from?"

"We used to ask *you* that," says Dad. "Who are you? Where did you come from? Why did you choose us?"

"We're all like foundlings, then."

"That's right," says Mum. "Little lost souls in a big big universe."

She smiles. She sighs.

"It's like it was intended," she says. "Like it was meant to be."

two

1

Mum photographs me. She gets close up to my skin. She gets the sunburn and the scarring. She gets the pores, the scars and nicks and bruises. She blows the photos up until they're like paintings, like weird landscapes. She photographs my elbows, my knees, and the scabs there become like massive outgrowths on an alien world. She does sections of hair, a nostril, an earlobe, a knuckle. She makes them four feet wide.

One day I'm lying in the garden with Max. Mum comes out.

She frames us with her fingers. She says how great we look. She tells Max she'd love to photograph him.

"No thanks," he says. "Sorry, Mrs. Lynch."

I say it's fine, it's just a game, there's nothing weird about it. Maybe his skin'll hang in a gallery in Newcastle and people will say it's beautiful. But he just shakes his head again.

She smiles, goes back inside.

"It *is* weird," he says. "Stripping off so somebody can take pictures of you that won't even look like you."

"Course it's not," I say.

"It *is*," he tells me.

"Just like *I'm* weird?" I ask him.

He shrugs.

"And what's the *point* of it?" he says.

"Dunno. Mebbe it shows how weird we all are if you look closely enough."

"I'm not," he says.

We look at each other and look away.

"It's easy for *you*," he says. "You can do what you like. You'll always be the son of Patrick Lynch."

"All of us can do what we like."

"No we can't. You're stupid if you think so."

I run my fingers through my ragged hair. I pick at a scab on my arm till the blood starts running. I use my fingernail to write with the blood. I write on my chest: STUPID. Max watches, shakes his head.

"Sometimes," he says, "I think you'll end up *doing* something really stupid."

I just laugh.

"That'll be your dad talking, is it?" I say. "I bet he's saying, 'Watch that Lynch lad. He'll go off the rails.'"

Max doesn't deny it. He stands up and heads off home.

I go into the house, into the kitchen with STUPID still scrawled on me. Dad's there with a coffee in his hand. He's staring out into the fields.

He jumps like I've woken him up.

"Imprinting!" he says.

"What?"

"There's this thing called imprinting. You can do it with lots of birds. But the raven's best of all. You get an egg just before it hatches. You make sure you're right there when it hatches. You make sure you're the first living creature the young bird sees. You stay with it. You give it its first food. And it attaches itself to you. It falls in love with you. It thinks you're its mother, its father. And it'll be yours forever. It'll follow you anywhere."

His eyes are wide and shining.

"So . . . ?" I say.

"So don't you see? Maybe the raven that took you to the baby had been imprinted. Maybe it was following someone, not leading you at all."

"Someone? The walker with the red hat, you mean."

"That's it! Maybe it was the walker with the red hat that was really leading you."

I stare at him. Could it be true?

"And yes!" he says. "Yes! Maybe the walker with the red hat was the mother! You said it was maybe a woman. She didn't want to show you herself where the baby was. She wanted her raven to lead you there and then she ran off!"

Could it be true?

"So where is she now?" I say.

"Dunno."

"And who's the father?"

"Dunno. Some barmy Northumbrian farmer. Something like that."

He stares into space, then at me.

"What's that?" he suddenly says.

He's pointing at my chest. I look down at the word in blood.

"Blood," I say.

"Your blood?"

"Yes."

"Whole books have been written about it, Liam," he says. "In the past, lots of old country folk had imprinted ravens of their own."

I think back to the walk through the village. I see the raven, I see the walker with the red hat. Could it be true?

"It seems like magic, but it's absolutely natural. It's like what we're doing with Alison. We feed her, we look after her. She behaves as if we're her parents and we behave as if we're her parents, but we're not."

He stares again, like he's trying to work it all out.

"So are you writing about it?" I say.

He laughs, then he purses his lips.

"Maybe," he says. "You know I can't talk about a story I'm in the middle of."

He punches the air.

"Imprinting!" he says. "It's so obvious. The woman with the red hat was the mother. The father's a daft old farmer." He grins. "What a story!"

Mum comes in as we're standing there. She has the baby in her arms.

Dad goes up close. He widens his eyes and leans right down over the baby's face.

"Hello, little lovely," he says. "I am your father. You are my child."

He kisses her, then he leaves.

"Yes!" he says as he climbs the stairs. "That's the answer!"

"What's the answer?" says Mum.

I shake my head.

She points at my chest.

"And much more interestingly, what's that?"

"Blood," I say.

She gets her camera out.

2

Mum frames the weirdest-looking photographs and takes them to her gallery. They love them, they say they're things of beauty. They hang them up for sale. We all go to see them, and it's so strange, looking at bits of myself hanging up in public view. Mum's simply called them *Landscape 1, Landscape 2*, etc.; and they don't look human at all. A couple of them have already been sold. Soon we'll be hanging in strangers' houses, weird and nameless and unrecognizable.

She photographs more and more. She photographs Alison's perfect skin. She takes Alison out in her buggy along the tracks and across the fields. Photographs cracked bark and cracked earth and sluggishly flowing water. Grasses and fungi. Dead moles hanging in a line on a fence. A pair of magpies strangled with wire. A rabbit with its throat ripped out. Three dried-out toads nailed to an oak tree. She photographs the living things and the dead things and the things that have never lived at all. She photographs the huge wild landscapes of Northumberland, the strange curved patterns of the rock art. The Roman Wall, the fortified farmhouses, the castles and bastles and peel towers and watchtowers, all the remnants of ancient vicious wars. The battlefields at Heavenfield and Flodden Field, where the grass blows in the breeze and tourists ramble and crops grow and sheep graze above hundreds upon hundreds of the dead. The beautiful vicious jets streak over her and through many of her pictures.

We watch the news about Iraq and the absence of news about Greg Armstrong. Bodies are stretchered away from bombed-out marketplaces, hauled out of devastated buses. Screaming parents carry their butchered children. They lift them into blankets and baskets. Men and women scrabble at bloodstained rubble in search of their loved ones beneath. Dad yells at the screen. Get the troops out! Blair! Bush! Suicide bombers! Terrorists! He thumps the air in frustration. They're all savages! They're all the bloody same!

Mum cries as she watches. She says, Yes they are all the same. All of them are people, just like us. She says it's happened always and everywhere. She says it happened here in the times of the border wars and the sheep raids, in the moors and fields and castles that bring the ramblers and the tourist coaches. Here was a place of terror and slaughter and death. And it could happen again if the circumstances are right, if the savages among us are let loose. There are savages everywhere, waiting their chance.

73

"We have to nurture the parts of us that aren't savage," she says. "We have to help the angel in us overcome the beast."

She holds Alison close and says that every body is like a baby's body, no matter how grown-up the person seems to be or tries to be. The body is soft, beautiful, vulnerable. It's easy to threaten it. It's easy to harm it. It takes next to nothing to cause pain, to draw blood, to break bones. Takes next to nothing to blast a body to bits. She hugs me and she hugs the baby. It's much harder to protect it, she says, and much more important. She takes us out into the fields and lanes. The trees are turning, birds are leaving, the days are shortening, darkening. She says that the tiniest corner of the countryside can stand for the whole world, no matter how peaceful and how isolated it might seem to be. It is gorgeous and strange and terrible and filled with throbbing life and awful death all at once. She goes to Rook Hall again and again. She photographs its walls, its rubble. There's a notice attached to the hall now. It's headed ABANDONED CHILD. There's a true photograph of Alison, and details of her discovery. There's a telephone number. Anyone with information should call it. Mum turns over stones, seeking for clues. She stands dead still, as if there might somehow be an answer to the mysteries in the atmosphere and air. Alison sits in the buggy and watches the flitting birds and gurgles and giggles with delight.

3

Mum says we should have Alison christened.

"You're joking!" says Dad.

It's dark outside. The baby's asleep upstairs. Dad's scribbling in a notebook.

"It's mumbo jumbo," he says. "And when was the last time you stepped foot in a church?"

"At your dad's funeral, but what's that got to do with it?"

Dad slaps his notebook shut.

"Do you know what christening's about? It's about saying that little kids like Alison are born with sin and evil in them. It's about washing away the evil in their souls. Now, tell me this: do you believe that Alison was born with evil in her?"

Mum shrugs. She sips her wine. Dad continues.

"And it's also about dedicating her life to God. Now, it'll come as a surprise to me if you believe in any God at all. So you'd be dedicating an innocent little child to a nonexistent phantom. And if I'm not mistaken, we didn't get *him* christened, did we?"

He points at me.

"And do *you* feel evil?" he asks me. "Do you feel like your sins haven't been washed away?"

I laugh.

"I feel like a perfect little angel, Daddy."

"Oh, aye?" he says.

"I know all that," says Mum. "But it's also about marking her arrival in the world. It's about welcoming her here."

"And for all we know," says Dad, "she might already be christened. She might be a Buddhist or a Moslem or a Seventh-Day blooming Adventist or a Tenth-Day Birk or some other wacky mumbo-jumbo sectist."

Mum sips her wine.

"How can she be anything?" she says. "She's just a little girl, and I think we should say, Welcome to our world."

Dad groans, shakes his head, heads upstairs.

"Have you seen how big his bum's getting?" she says. She giggles.

"It's a writer's hazard. He's hardly moved for weeks. So what do you think about the christening?"

I shrug.

"Don't really care," I say.

"I'll go and see the vicar tomorrow, then. Any idea what his name is?"

76

"Haven't a clue."

She peers at me.

"We could get you done at the same time, if you like," she says.

"No thanks. I'll just stay evil."

4

It happens at St. Michael and All Angels. The little chapel is in a field on a ridge above the village. It's a Sunday afternoon. You can see for miles, all the pastures and empty moors of Northumberland stretching north. A few farmhouses. The scattered villages—Chilton, Wark, Bellington, Otterburn. The castles—Highton, Swinburn, Simonhope, Chase—tucked away in valleys and copses. The ruins of Rook Hall, and a dozen other ruins crumbling into the earth. The wilderness of moorland to the north, the dark bulges of the Cheviots far off, the limits of vision before Scotland starts. Sheep lie dozing in the little graveyard. Rooks caw. Motorbikes roar on the military road. A train clatters and hoots down in the Tyne Valley. The low-flying jets, again and again and again.

Joe Tynan comes with a camera crew from ITV. Friends from

the village and from Newcastle are there. Max and his big family are there. Jack Scott and his crowd are there. Social workers. WPC Jenkins and PC Ball, without their bulletproof vests this time. Doreen the paramedic. How could they *not* come? they all say. They couldn't stay away. And here come Phil and Phil, and Crystal and Oliver. They laugh and cluster about us and lean close to Alison and they bill and coo and smile and smile.

Crystal's hair is gelled into loops and curls. Her green eyes shine in her face that's caked with white makeup. She's wearing safety pins in her ears, woven multicolored elastic bands around her neck.

"I knew we'd meet again," she says. "It's the baby. She's the link. And it's all just fate. Do you believe in fate?"

"I don't know."

"Sometimes things are meant to happen. You were meant to find the baby. The baby was meant to lead you to me and to Oliver. What happens next is meant to happen."

She laughs.

"Or maybe it's all just nonsense. And nothing's meant at all. And things happen just because they happen. Can I write to you?"

"Write to me?"

"Just e-mails. Just to keep in touch."

She scribbles an e-mail address on a piece of card and gives it to me.

"We're one family," says the vicar when the service starts. "We're drawn together by a child who was abandoned, who was lost. But she's also any baby, every baby. She's every single one of us." He glances shyly at Dad. "I will, if I may, quote the poet William Blake." Dad groans quietly. The vicar recites:

"Into the dangerous world I leapt,
Helpless, naked, piping loud."

He pauses.

"Isn't that all of us," he says. "Into the dangerous world we leap. All of us are waifs and foundlings. And all of us need love. Love, and family, and trust in God."

Dad groans. The vicar lowers his voice.

"Do I dare," he whispers, "make the connection between this child and Jesus in his manger?"

"Please, no," breathes Dad.

The vicar opens the service book.

"Perhaps not," he says. "But I leave the thought to linger. Now, let us welcome this precious child into our world."

We take the baby to the font. The vicar pours water on her. He drives all evil out. Mum's friend Sue is godmother. Dad's agent, Nick Stone, is godfather. We all promise to protect her, to bring her up in faith, to resist the devil and all his works.

Our hymns echo off the walls and out into the surrounding spaces.

Jesus bids us shine
In a pure clear light
Like a little candle
Burning in the night.
In this world of darkness
We must shine,
You in your small corner,
And I in mine.

80

5

Afterwards there's a party in the house and the garden. Dad
sits on a garden bench with Nick Stone drinking whisky. I
stand and listen. Dad's telling Nick about imprinting, about
ravens. He says imprinting must happen with humans, too.
The very first seconds of life must be crucial to all of us. So
where does that leave foster parents? Is it too late for imprinting, even when the child is still a baby? And what about older
kids, like the lad from Liberia?

"So are you writing about this?" says Nick.

"Kind of," says Dad. He laughs. "I'm writing about a
barmy farmer and a country lass and their secret child. Oh,
and their raven." He winks at me. "Liam understands, don't
you, son?"

"Do I?" I say.

"But what about the book you were writing?" says Nick.

"I'll go back to it," says Dad.

"But what about your schedule?"

Dad shrugs.

"I'll get back to it," he says.

Nick sighs.

"And another thing," says Dad. "What happens if your first parents are taken away and replaced by a monster? Will you love the monster and follow the monster? And can you get back to the first imprinting?" He ponders. "But that's probably a different story."

"So you're writing two books?"

"Or maybe three."

"You got a title?" says Nick.

"Nope."

Nick sighs, smiles at me, swigs his whisky. I move on.

Mum passes the baby from one guest to the other. They bill and coo and say how beautiful she is and what a treasure she is. Mum takes visitors to see her paintings and photographs. I see her whispering in a corridor with Jack Scott. He's in jeans, a red shirt, his hair's short and sharp. She laughs with him, low and soft. I turn away just as they're about to kiss.

Phil and Phil have both lost weight. Philip drinks white wine and nibbles carrots and celery sticks.

"I'm a changed man," he announces. "Just had me whatdeyecallit and I'm fit as a lop!"

"Your ECG," says Philomena.

"And soon we're off to California," says Phil.

"*California?*" says Mum.

"Aye. It's what we've always wanted: San Francisco, San Diego, Sacrawhatdeyecallit."

"Sacramento," says Philomena.

"Aye. Not yet, they say. But we'll be gone soon. Straight to San Fran. Then the Chevy all the way down Highway One."

At dusk I go down the garden with Max and Oliver and Crystal. The tent's there, by the fire pit.

"We sleep out in it," I say.

Crystal runs her fingers across the canvas. She says it's beautiful. She laughs.

"You're a dreamer, aren't you," she says. "You're a wild boy, Liam."

We light a fire in the fire pit and sit by it on logs and stones. Soon there's a gap of darkness between the party and us.

Oliver's in a new foster home now. So's Crystal. They see each other at weekends. They sit together, lean against each other. Oliver puts his arm around her.

"This is a strange land," says Oliver. "When I thought of England, the pictures in my head were of Tower Bridge, Buckingham Palace, Bath, the fields of Kent. Not this space, not all these empty places."

An owl screeches somewhere close by. A few bats are out, flickering through the limits of the firelight—late flights before they go back into hibernation. Crystal hums a tune as she leans against him. She leans forward to stir the fire with a stick.

"They've said they think he'll be safe," she says.

"In Liberia?" I say.

"Aye, in Liberia."

"I will die," says Oliver. "I will be slaughtered."

"*Slaughtered?*" says Max.

"Like a beast. Like my mother, my father, like my sisters, my brothers."

Crystal stirs the fire again. The sparks rise and dance. The fire simmers, crackles, creaks.

"Some stories are beyond belief," she says. "But they're the truest and oldest stories of them all. Tell them, Ollie."

He pauses. He collects his thoughts.

"They came one morning," says Oliver. "A troupe of them with rifles and axes and clubs." He waves away the sparks that rise. He sighs. "Some of them were children, just like me, children with weapons in their fists, children with murder in their eyes. Can you believe that?"

He pauses. He waits.

"*Can* you?" says Crystal.

Her eyes glitter in the firelight and her hair and her face glow.

"You *have to* believe it," she says. "Any one of us could be a murderer if they got us early enough. The murderer in all of us is just below the skin."

Max sighs.

"Who's *they*?" he says.

"*They*," says Crystal, "are the beasts of the world. *They* are the ones that were turned into beasts by the beasts that went before."

Max shrugs. Maybe he doesn't want to know. Maybe he doesn't want to think these things.

"You," says Crystal, "might think you are an angel, but you're *not*. What you got is food and money and safety and parents that love you. But what if you *didn't* have them things? What if your parents were—"

Oliver hushes her. He puts his finger to her lips.

"Tell them more," she says.

"Imagine this," he says to us. "Imagine Liberia. Imagine me, not as I am now, but as a child, a little boy. Indeed, I have food, I have parents that love me, and I am happy, until this day. I am lying in the long grass close to my family home. The earth is warm, the sun is beating down on me. I am lying there to hide, because the soldiers have come to our village. For a long time we have feared that they will come. We have been certain that they will come. We have heard all the tales of what happens when they come. We have even played games about this, my friends and I. We have lain in the long grass and we have held sticks as if they were guns. We have imagined fighting for our village, driving the soldiers away. But now the soldiers are here and I am very frightened and there is no way that they can be driven away. I lie trembling in the long grass as the soldiers take my family, and another family, out into the fields. They give them rakes and spades. They point guns at them. 'Dig your graves,' they command. 'Dig your graves!' And my mother and my father and my sister and my brother dig their graves. And the soldiers stand close by, laughing and smoking cigarettes. Then they raise their guns and they slaughter my family."

No one by the fireside dares to speak. The voices drift across the garden from the house.

Oliver looks into our faces.

"I have no evidence of what happened. I do not even have evidence of who I am." He points to his head, his heart. "The evidence is here, and here. And in my writing, in which I try to tell the truth. They say I cannot stay here. I am not angry that they say this. You cannot accept everyone into your country."

He looks across the fire.

"I am Oliver Part. I am thirteen years old. I am from Liberia. My family was slaughtered. I ran away. I will not ask if you believe. It does not matter what anyone believes. I know the truth, and I try to tell it, and the truth is difficult."

"What will you do?" I say.

His wide eyes shine as he looks across the flames.

"I will not go back."

"We'll fly," says Crystal. "We'll run. We'll hide. They won't find us."

Across the garden, someone plays the Northumbrian pipes, a slow soft tune. Then there's a shadow, and footsteps in the grass. Nattrass. His face looms into the light.

"Gotcha!" he says.

He grins. No one speaks.

"Just popped in to wish the baby well," he says.

His face twists, somewhere between a grimace and a grin.

"The land's full of strangers today," he says. "You gonna introduce me, brother?"

I'm about to tell him to shove off. Crystal stands up. She steps across the flames towards him. She raises her arm and points at him.

"Who are *you*?" she says. "What do *you* want?"

"I'm Gordon Nattrass, sister," he says.

He puts his hand out. She doesn't take it.

"I am not your sister," she replies.

"But we're all one big and happy human family," he says.

He looks down at Oliver. "Welcome to Northumberland, brother." He doesn't put his hand out. Oliver nods, murmurs a greeting in reply.

Crystal leans closer to Nattrass.

"Go away," she says.

Philip calls from the house: "Crystal! Oliver! We have to go!"

"Crystal," hisses Nattrass. "And Oliver."

His eyes glitter as he laughs at Crystal.

"I'll remember you," he says. "Farewell."

He turns back into the night.

Crystal stands at the edge of the firelight, watching him go.

"Friend of yours?" asks Crystal.

"We hate him," I say.

"Good!"

Philip calls again. We stand up.

"If there's anything we can do . . . ," I say to Oliver.

His eyes shine brightly again.

"I will think of you as my friend. And you as well, Max."

Crystal comes to me.

"You'll help him," she whispers. "I know you will. You're good and strong. I know you are."

She kisses my cheek, then starts back with Oliver towards the house.

As we walk back, Mum appears with her camera.

"Just one shot," she says. "You look so strange and so lovely, coming through the darkness together with the lights in your eyes and the fire burning behind."

We stand still and face her. I stand at Crystal's side.

Afterwards, Max holds me back for a moment.

"Do you *believe* it?" he says.

"Believe what?"

"All that stuff. All that slaughter."

I pull away and look at him.

"Course I do," I say.

I stumble back towards the party.

"The world's a savage place, you know," I say.

"You're such an innocent," I say.

6

A couple of days later I pass Nattrass in the village.

"Who's the terrorist?" he says.

"The what?"

"The black lad. Whatsisname."

"Oliver."

I start to move on.

"Aye, him. What's he done? And what's he doing here? And what's he gonna do?"

"He's from Liberia. He's looking for asylum."

"Thought so."

"And he's not here. He's in Newcastle."

"Best place for him. They'll know what to do with him."

I start to move again, but I turn back.

"You haven't got a clue, have you?"

He grins.

"Have I not, brother?"

"No, you haven't. Terrible things have happened to Oliver. Things that you and me couldn't imagine."

"And you believe him, don't you? Course you do. Peace and joy and love and let them all come in." He laughs. "You're a pushover. Half of them's war criminals, man. They're here to avoid justice. They're terrorists." He makes a fist and thumps the air. "Send them back to their hovels! Bomb them back to the Stone Age!"

He grins again.

"Just joking," he says. "Pal of yours, is he?"

"Yes," I say.

"Thought so. That's great. Great to have pals from all round the world. Universal love and joy. How else we gonna have peace and understanding." He grins, then narrows his eyes. "Oh, and just one more thing, Liam. I *can* imagine, you know."

He looks at me, like he's daring me to deny it.

"I always remember that day your dad come into school, Liam. Remember? That day he was reading to us from his books and talking to us and getting us to write stuff down. Aye?"

It was a couple of years back. Dad still liked to go into schools then. To get feedback, he used to say. To inspire the new generation of readers and writers. It was part of his duty as a writer.

"One thing always sticks in me mind," says Nattrass. "It was truly inspiring. All of us, he said, *all* of us have got the

90

most amazing imaginations. D'you remember, Liam? Each and every one of us."

"It's what he always says."

"Well, it's absolutely true. Me, I can imagine *anything*. I can imagine the worst things in the whole wide world. Sometimes I amaze myself with the things that's going on inside my brain. Sometimes, Liam, I can scare meself stiff." He laughs. "Whatsisname's tale, for instance. That'd be a piece of cake for a brain like mine. Blood and guts and savagery and slaughter. Dear me, it's horrible just to think of it. See you around, brother."

And we move on.

7

I e-mail Crystal. I don't know what to say.

> Good to see you at the christening. Hope
> everything's OK.
> Best, Liam

She replies almost immediately.

> It was good to see you again. It was great at the fire,
> eyes shining and skin glowing and the way our voices
> sounded in the crackle of the flames. We got to think of
> Oliver. Will you be ready to help him when he needs
> you? I'm in my little room. The sky is red and orange like
> a fire blazing bright above the roofs. The whole world is

still. We all wait for the grate thing to happen. Will it be
a thing of terror or a thing of marvel? Sorry if I seem
intens. It is how I am tonight. Night night.
Cx

I imagine her in the city, in her little room, staring out into
the fiery night. I imagine her pale face, her green eyes. I check
again before I sleep.

When you came into our home it was like we had been
waiting for you. It was like I had known you always. It
was like we would definitely meet again and definitely
have to go through something together. Did you feel
that too Liam? Cx

I think back to the foster home. I think of their eyes on me.
I think of the knife scar on Oliver's face. I think of Crystal
close beside me at the table. And I think of Alison, how I found
her, how she went away, how I went to her again and found
her foster sister and her foster brother. It was almost like she
led me to them, just like the raven led me to her. And I think
that yes, maybe this has all been intended.

I think I know what you mean. I do feel something too.
I don't understand it.
Lx

Understanding doesnt mater.
Cx

8

Still hot, but the days start to shorten. The darkening nights intensify our games. We play football until we can't see the ball. We go on with our war games, we creep in the shadows, we ambush each other with savage cries. We wrestle and scream. We play Spotlight.

Spotlight. The bay's in the middle of the field, the stump of an old chestnut tree. We play when the stars of the vivid Northumbrian night are beginning to shine. When you're It you take the torch. You stand at the bay. You close your eyes. You count as the others scatter into the ditches and trenches and hedges and copses all around. Then you switch on the torch and go searching, pointing the beam of light into the furthest fringes of the dark. You see a hiding figure. *I see you!* you call. And then you run, chased by the one who was hiding, and you thump the bay and cry, *Spotlight spotted you in the night! You're out!* When you hide, curled up as if you're dead on the hard earth or tangled in a hawthorn or balanced on a beech bough, you feel you're far far away, in your own little isolated world. You hear the chanted counting ringing out across the field. You hear the grunts and stifled laughter of the others hiding. Then there's the cry: *The counting's all done and here I come!* You peep out. You see the cone of light dipping and swinging and searching. You hear the cries: *Spotlight spotted you in the night! You're out!* You hear the frantic running. You see the torch beam whipping wildly as its holder runs. And you wait for the beam to come to you at last, to dazzle you, to get you springing into speed and life again.

One night during Spotlight I'm deep in a ditch in the darkest shadows when Nattrass slithers in beside me.

"Aye, aye, brother," he whispers. "Mind if I share your ditch?"

I try to shift away from him, but we're crammed close together.

"I could do you now and nobody'd know who it was," he whispers.

He holds up a knife. It shines in the moonlight.

"I could, couldn't I?" he says.

"Yes," I sigh.

He laughs. He holds the blade to my throat. I push it away. He holds it to my throat again.

"Come on," he says. "Fight me off."

"Piss off," I tell him.

"Dangerous thing to say to somebody with a knife at your throat," he says.

I feel the edge of the blade on my skin. I lie there, tense, still.

"One wrong little move and you'd be gone," he whispers.

But he takes the knife away, and laughs softly.

"Just joking, brother," he says. "You know that, don't you?" He laughs.

"I like to keep you on your toes, that's all."

I look past him, see the torch beam swerving through the dark.

"I found a video on the Net today," Nattrass whispers. "I seen a man getting his head chopped off. It was a piece of cake to find."

The torch beam sweeps across us, doesn't shine down into the ditch.

"They said the bloke was evil," he continues. "They said he was against God. They said that what they were doing was for God. Then they got a knife, a great big one . . ."

"It wasn't Greg Armstrong, was it?"

"No, some Frenchie or a Kraut. So there's still a bit of hope for poor old Greg."

"Why you telling me?" I say.

He laughs.

"Haven't a clue. Mebbe I want to shock you, Liam. Mebbe I want to scare you a little bit. Mebbe I want to get you imagining the worst things in the world."

"I don't need you for that," I tell him.

He grunts, grins. "They held his head right up in front of the camera. Hey, even I had to look away."

His skin gleams in the starlight.

"You think I'm a pain in the neck," says Nattrass. "You think I'm weird. You even think I might be evil."

I don't say anything. I listen. I wait for the torch to find us.

"I'm not, you know," he says. "I'm just me, and I'm like lots of other folk. Mebbe a bit dafter, a bit wilder, that's all."

"Is that right?"

"Aye, that's right. There's lots like me. Why d'you think they put them videos on the Net? Cos they know there's millions wanting to see them."

"And millions that don't."

"Ha! Think about when you go to the flicks, Liam. When you're sitting in the dark down at the Forum watching a film. What happens at the violent bits, eh? At the really savage bits. Like the last James Bond film when Bond smashes that guy's head on the washbasin and there's the crunch of bone and the splattering of blood and he goes on smashing him till the washbasin's all smashed up as well. You hear it, don't you? And you even—don't you?—hear them *laugh*. That's what I'm on about."

"That means nothing," I say. "A movie's all made up. The video you saw was—"

"Real. Aye. But you don't get it, do you? There's no difference. Aye, you watch the picture with loads of others in the Forum. And aye, you watch the beheading all alone. But while you're watching it in secret, you know you're watching with a million others all around the world."

He holds up the knife again and turns it so that it glows in the moonlight. I think of Death Dealer, resting in a drawer in my bedroom. I could do you, too, I think. I smile at the vision of it, of Nattrass stretched out dead on the icy earth like an ancient fighter, with Death Dealer thrust into his heart.

"It's a vicious world, Liam. And you know why? Cos people love it that way. Cos all of us are beasts at heart. Your new mate, whatdeyecallim, he'll know all about that. And so do you, Liam Lynch."

And he prods me in the chest with the knife point. Once. Twice. I feel it through my clothes.

"Don't you," he says. "Even you. Don't you? You know all about getting wild. We seen it with the snakes that day, didn't we?"

He prods me.

"Go on," he says. "Have a go at me. Go on. Go on."

I punch him in the face. I snarl at him to shut up. He laughs and stabs the knife at me again. I grip his wrist and try to twist the knife back towards him. We wrestle. The knife gleams right by my face. He's stronger than me but he's holding back. He's grinning. The knife comes closer. Then he jumps free.

"Whoops!" he laughs. "Get running, Liam!"

The torch beam glares into my eyes. I jump up, sprint, don't get back in time.

Spotlight spotted you in the night! You're out!

9

That night I dream of Nattrass. We're fighting on the field. We struggle for hour after hour. I think it will never end, but at last I plunge Death Dealer into his heart. I stand over him as his blood leaks out into the earth. Next morning, I see the horizontal cut on my cheek. Shallow, just a couple of inches long. A dark red line of dried blood. I close my eyes. I dream again of plunging the knife into his heart.

At breakfast, Mum reaches out, touches it.

"What's that?"

I feel the line.

"Hawthorn tree," I say.

"Hawthorn?"

"I was hiding. I ran into the tree. A thorn got me."

She gets her camera.

10

Crystal continues to e-mail.

I wasn't always with Phil and Phil. There's been others.
Mr. and Mrs. Pearson were best of all. They had a lovely
house with a pretty garden and a little pond with
goldfish and a cherry tree and a dog called Sam. There
was a skyblue canopy across my bed and a dream
catcher to catch bad dreams. They were teachers. They
were about to love me very much. They wanted to make
me so happy. They said I was the girl that they had
always wanted. They wanted to adopt me.
So I got a knife and I cut myself, up high on my arm
beside my shoulder. There was blood on my sheets. And

on my pillow. Not much, just a trickle and some spots. But enough to scare them off.

I write to you because I don't know anybody like you, anybody normal. And I think you and me and Ol were meant to meet.

Cx

11

There's a big gathering in Hexham for Greg Armstrong. It starts with prayers outside the abbey. I'm standing beside Max and Kim. Becky Smith's on the other side of them. I take no notice of her. Prayers are led by a vicar, a priest, a rabbi and a muezzin. I don't join in. Afterwards we all head towards the marketplace, where a little stage has been put up. A few old hippies are singing "We Shall Overcome."

"There's no harm in praying, you know," says Max as we move towards the stage.

"There's no good in it, either," I say. "What's God going to do to get anybody free? And if he can do it, why hasn't he started by now?"

"It's better than doing nothing," Max says. "It's as good as singing along with that wrinkly lot."

"Is it?"

I see Kim and Becky are trying to hear what we're saying. I raise my voice. "Maybe it's God that's the problem," I say. "If there *is* a God, maybe we should be praying to him to get himself down here right now and explain himself. Because if there *is* a God, he's the biggest war criminal of them all." I check to hear that Becky's listening. "And anyway, there isn't a God. He's dead, he's gone, there's only us."

Greg's wife's on the stage. She appeals to his captors. Poets step up and read their poems.

Kids from school carry homemade banners.

SET GREG FREE

GIVE PEACE A CHANCE

TROOPS OUT NOW

We keep clapping our hands and stamping our feet and chanting the words. I yell louder than anyone.

Dad steps up. He reads a page from something he's working on. Mum and I stare at each other when he quotes her own words.

"We all have the capacity to harm," he says. "But we have to transcend that capacity. We have to help the angel in us to overcome the beast. Or we are doomed."

I hold Alison for a while. She smiles and giggles and loves it all. Everyone sings "Blowin' in the Wind" and she moves in my arms to the rhythm.

Becky slides past Kim. I shift away.

"Are you avoiding me?" she says.

I put a sneer on my face.

"Why would I be avoiding *you*?" I say.

She tickles the baby's chin.

"Oh," she says. "Your big brother is such a toughie, such a weirdo!"

She walks away.

Nattrass passes by with Eddie and Ned. They stand watching the stage, grinning. They link arms, they sway, they start dancing like there's a barn dance going on, winding and twisting their way through the crowd. .

Nattrass chants:

"A-one two three, one two three, Down with *evil*! A-one two three, one two three, Down with *death*!"

12

There's an e-mail from a name I don't recognize. I want to click it away, but it says *For Liam Lynch, the Foundling Kid.* I grit my teeth and open it. There's an attachment. I open that as well. A video begins.

The picture's blurry. There's a figure sitting on a chair at the center of a small poorly lit room. He's wearing jeans and a striped shirt and there's a black hood covering his head. His head's tilted forward, like he's asleep. Music's playing: a beaten drum, a scratchy squeaky stringed instrument. There's some chanting. None of the words are recognizable. Three figures walk into view. They're small, with padded jackets on, with full face masks on, circles for eyeholes, slits for mouth and nose. They stand around the man on the chair—one at his back, one at each side—and they face the camera. They hold the man's shoulders as if to restrain him. The figure at his back has a piece of paper. He unfolds it and begins to read in a grunty guttural weird voice. Again hardly anything's recognizable: *Jabber jabber jabber God jabber jabber jabber Allah jabber jabber jabber Blair jabber jabber jabber Bush.* It goes on for a couple of minutes. The man on the chair doesn't move. The men at his side stare into the camera. The man at the back closes the paper, drops it. He goes, *Jabber jabber jabber death.* I click Pause. I can't go on. Lean back from the computer screen and breathe. Look around my room, my ordinary world. Look out of the window into cold, empty Northumberland. Breathe deeply and click Play again. The man at the back has a long-bladed knife. I lean right back, grit my teeth, hold my head, but I watch. Can it be real? Surely not. It's just not possible, is it? The man on the chair just sits there. He hardly moves as the man at his back leans over him with the knife. The picture goes all blurry. When the picture clears, the man with the knife is lifting the head free of the body. He takes the hood off it. It's a pig's head, staring out of the screen. The body beneath is a scarecrow. The men are teenagers, hooting with the thrill of it. They're teenagers, just like me. Then they're gone, the screen's blank.

I lean back, then I curse.

"Nattrass."

I pause and play, pause and play. I run it in slow motion. I watch closely, to see the boys behind the masks, the scarecrow behind the clothes, the pig behind the hood. Listen to hear the voices within the mumbo jumbo.

"Nattrass."

"Well, even them that say they don't like the violent stuff—like you, for instance . . ."

"What about me?"

"You watch it. You can't stop. You—"

"It was stupid," I say.

"Stupid? Ah, well. That's what they say about lots of this modern art, isn't it?"

"Art?"

"Aye, art. They call it stupid, meaningless. Absolutely shocking, man! Shouldn't be allowed!"

He swings the hammer down and lets the head thud onto the pavement.

"Some people took it for real, you know," he says. "Couldn't tell the difference. They thought it truly was some barmy terrorist thing, that there was some message in the pig's head. I knew you wouldn't be fooled. You, with your background. I knew *you'd* know what's real and what's not real. That's why I was wanting a word with you, Liam. Well, with your mother, really."

"My mother?"

"Aye. I was thinking of them galleries. The ones she puts them pictures in."

"What about them?"

"Well, they do that video art these days, don't they?"

He laughs again.

"And I was thinking. Mebbe I could put some of my stuff in. What do you think?"

I roll my eyes.

"Aye," I say. "Maybe you should. Maybe you're a brilliant and talented artist."

"Exactly what I was thinking, brother. So mebbe I should have a word with her, eh? What do you think she'd say?"

"I think she'd say piss off, Nattrass."

"Get away. She uses language like that, does she? I'm shocked! Ah, well. Mebbe I should talk to somebody else, then. One of that arty lot at the brat's christening. They look like they'd know the real stuff if they saw it, eh?"

"Aye," I say. "Whatever, Nattrass."

I move on. His laughter follows me.

"Hey, Liam!" he shouts. "Watch out for more. There's shootings, beatings, stonings, lots more stuff we can get to work on. Did you see that Saddam Whatsisname getting hanged? That'd be easy to do, man! That'd be a piece of cake. That'd be a proper work of art!"

A week later there's another video. A man walks up some steps in a barn. A hood is put onto his head. A noose is put around his neck. A trapdoor opens and he plummets to his death.

Then there's a hand scribbling blood-colored ink onto white paper.

Yes. I can imagine anything.
ANYTHING!

by
The Gnat

Then Mum's calling from downstairs.

"Liam! Phone call for you!"

15

A woman's voice, urgent.

"Is that Liam? Liam Lynch?"

"Yes."

"You're a friend of Crystal's?"

"Yes."

"Forgive me. I'm Crystal's foster mum. I'm Marjorie Stone. I'm contacting people she might have been in touch with."

I know what's coming. I watch the baby. She's in a high chair at the table, with a bowl of mashed-up vegetables in front of her.

"She's disappeared, Liam," says Mrs. Stone. "Night before last. Wasn't in her bed yesterday morning."

Mum's eyes ask: *Who is it? What's happening?*

"And her friend," says Mrs. Stone. "Oliver, the Liberian

boy. Him as well." Her voice catches. She's crying. "She hasn't been with us long. It happens all the time, kids running off from foster homes. But she's young. Have you . . ."

I see the police car through the kitchen window. It's coming down the lane. It pulls up outside the house.

"Have you heard anything?" says Mrs. Stone. "She likes you, she talked about you. Has she been in touch?"

"No. No."

Mum goes to the door. I watch PC Ball and WPC Jenkins coming, straightening their bulletproof vests.

"But you'll tell us," says Mrs. Stone. "If she does get in touch, you'll let us know."

"Yes. Of course."

I put the phone down. The police officers come into the kitchen.

"Hello, son," says PC Ball. He winks. "Found any bairns recently?"

I ignore his joke.

"That was Crystal's foster mother," I say to Mum. "She's run away. With Oliver."

"So what do you know?" says Ball.

"Me? Nothing."

"He hardly knows them," says Mum.

"Seems they knew him, though," says Ball. "Very fond of him, they were, by all accounts, so here we are." He takes a notebook out of his pocket. "So. Where d'you think they might have gone?"

"I've no idea."

He shrugs.

"None at all? They said nothing, talked about nothing?"

"No. Nothing."

"Ah, well. Worth a try, eh?"

He crouches beside the baby. She coos and smiles. The baby laughs and holds out a fistful of mash. Jenkins laughs.

"Funny how things happen round you," she says. "Foundling babies, runaway orphans, escaped asylum seekers. What's next?"

"It's like that with some folk," says Ball. "They attract stuff. Other folk—a life of peace and quiet and nothing at all."

Mum puts a cup of tea into his hand.

"You'll let us know, if anything turns up?"

"Course he will," says Mum.

"That's good."

They swig their tea. We hear Dad moving about upstairs, hear the printer whirring. Ball raises his eyebrows.

"Writer at work, eh? It must be great, having a dad that's a famous writer."

He holds his pen over his notebook, turns his eyes to the sky, pretends to write as if inspired.

"Ahem. I wandered lonely as a . . . Sorry." He closes the book. "Mind you, if I do ever get round to writing some of the things we've seen . . ."

"Bestseller stuff," says Jenkins.

"Aye. Bestseller stuff in ordinary town streets, bestseller stuff in peaceful villages. All looks peaceful and lovey-dovey till . . ." He pauses, looks at me closely, points to my cheek. "Had an accident, son?"

I touch the faint thin line there.

"A hawthorn tree," I say.

"Ha. Fun and games, eh? I thought you looked like you're enjoying the summer. Look how brown he is, eh?"

"Like a berry," says Jenkins. "And look at that hair. Like a wild boy."

"It's great, isn't it? You be wild while you can, son. The real world'll be at you soon enough."

He straightens his vest. They head for the door.

Ball turns and looks at me a last time.

"You won't keep it to yourself. If there is some news."

"Course he won't," says Jenkins. "He's a good citizen, this one. Aren't you, son?"

"Yes," I say.

"Course he is," says Ball. "There's no trouble in a nice young citizen like that."

They go to the car, drive back towards the village. The sun glints off the little police car with the shapes of bulletproofed police officers hunched inside.

"You've really heard nothing?" says Mum.

"Nothing."

She holds the baby's hand. She waves it.

"Bye-bye, nice policeman. Bye-bye, nice police lady."

16

Nothing strange about it. Kids are always running off from children's homes. Asylum seekers melt away. The world is full of tales of children lost in a big and scary world. They're the tales we tell to Alison before she sleeps.

Once there was a girl called Little Red Riding Hood. . . .

One day a pretty little girl called Goldilocks set off walking through the trees. . . .

Hansel was the brother and Gretel was the sister and they lived with their mummy and their daddy beside a big dark scary wood. . . .

*The news appears on TV for a moment—There's a girl called Crystal and a boy called Oliver and they disappeared in the night—*then it fades, as all news stories fade.

three

1

I climb into the chestnut tree in the field beside the school. I climb higher, higher. I spend an afternoon in it, scanning the countryside that leads to Newcastle. I see the military road and the Roman Wall stretching away towards the west. I see the chapel of St. Michael and All Angels on the ridge above the village. If they come, that's where they'll come from. I imagine them coming down through the fields, coming down on the footpath that runs alongside the wall. I'd know them immediately, the white girl, the black boy. I see nothing. Late afternoon I climb down, go home.

Mum's at the back door smoking a cigarette and swigging a big glass of wine.

"Hello, son," she says, but her mouth's all pursed and her eyes are bitter.

"What's up?" I say.

"Everything! Art."

"Art?"

Dad's behind her with a coffee in his hand.

"Your mum's just back from the gallery," he says.

A few of her framed photographs are leaning against the kitchen wall.

"I've been ditched," says Mum. "They don't want my work anymore."

"Yes, they do," says Dad. "You've still got four or five in there."

"I don't want them there! I don't want our lovely baby and our lovely son—"

"The *skin* of our lovely son."

"Whatever. But I don't want them hanging next door to that . . ."

Smoke seeps out between her teeth.

"That what?" I say.

"That . . . filth! That disgusting trashy . . . Yuck! Yuck yuck yuck!"

She glugs her wine. She drags on her cigarette, then flings it away.

"They have hung the most disgusting stuff on the walls. . . ."

"It's not even in the main gallery," says Dad. "It's that old warehousy place where they put all the weird stuff."

"Hangings!" says Mum. "Hangings and beheadings and stonings that turn out not to be real hangings and beheadings and stonings. Knives and blood and axes everywhere. Pigs' heads and beasts' hearts and snapped bones and crushed skulls . . . Ugh! Ugh!"

120

"So is it art?" says Dad.

"It's filth. What kind of pleasure can you get from watching it? What kind of twisted mind gets pleasure making it?"

Dad sips his coffee.

"Maybe it's not about pleasure," he says. "Maybe they're showing us how horrible the world is. Maybe they're exploring the nature of reality and illusion, truth and lies."

"Maybe they're just getting off on their own sordid tastes."

Dad shrugs.

"And maybe it's showing that we're all just a kind of meat in the end."

She glares at him.

"I'm not meat! You're not! Liam's not! Alison isn't!"

She glares at him, lights another cigarette. She glares at him again when he says she should put it out. She jabs him in the chest.

"Stop telling me what to do, mister!"

He sighs and looks at his watch. Time to head upstairs again.

"Who they by?" I ask.

"Nobody that'll put their name to them," says Mum. "They're by somebody that goes by the name of the Gnat. The *Gnat*! And they've put warnings about the content on the gallery door."

"What does whatsisname—Jack Scott—think of them?" says Dad.

She spits breath.

"Jack precious Scott! Oh, he thinks they're new and strange. He thinks they fit the times. He thinks they're at the cutting edge!"

121

"Maybe they are. Maybe they're exactly what people are looking for."

"People! Sickos and weirdos and people that like murder and mayhem and that's got not a clue about art."

"Maybe that's most people," says Dad.

Mum screams, short and sharp. She clamps her hands across her ears.

"I don't want to think that. I *can't* think that."

"But maybe it has to be thought. Maybe that's exactly why there's murder and mayhem. Because we love it. Because the desire for it is deep inside us."

"It's not in *me*!" says Mum. She jabs him hard in the chest again. "It's not in *me*!"

2

We all go to see. We leave Alison with little Mrs. Bolton al[ong]
the lane. We go to the gallery. It's got corrugated walls an[d]
corrugated roof. The lights are low. There are video screens [on]
the walls. I see the videos I know, or segments of them. T[he]
pig's head, dripping blood, is sawn off time and again.

One video just shows a torch moving through a dark spa[ce,]
the beam rising and falling, going away, then coming ba[ck]
again, like it's searching, like it's playing Spotlight, until [it]
rushes towards the camera, shines right towards the viewer.

"Gotcha!" says a growling sinister voice that I kn[ow]
straightaway. Then there's a hand thrusting a knife towar[ds]
you.

Other videos show a firing squad. Easy to see that the bo[d]-
ies are stuffing and straw, that the hooded heads are pi[g]

heads or sheep's heads or footballs or turnips. Easy to see the clumsy video cuts where real bodies are replaced with false.

"Maybe that's part of the point," says Dad. "Brutality's a game. Bodies are stuffing and straw. Human heads are pigs' heads."

"*Mine* isn't!" snaps Mum. She reaches out and cradles my head in her hands. She cradles Dad's head. "And yours isn't. And yours isn't."

There are hidden speakers with crackling voices, voices from radio reports of long-ago wars. Whispered accounts of ambushes and torture and abductions in the night. The noises of bullets and bombs and low-flying aircraft. Screams and howls and terrified appeals for mercy. Laughter and scorn.

It's like walking through a nightmare.

In the hanging video, the victim climbs the steps, is noosed, then drops, then climbs the steps again as if rising from his death, is noosed and drops again, again, again, again.

"So?" says Mum as we stand together watching it.

"Horrible," says Dad. "But hypnotic, you have to give it that."

Mum turns away.

"And it makes you think."

"Think of what?" says Mum.

"Of . . . Sisyphus," says Dad. "It makes you think of Christ on his cross."

"So you'd have it on the wall?"

"No. But—"

"But nothing. It's voyeuristic trash. Anybody could do it! Anybody with a camera and a computer and a twisted-enough brain!"

The victim drops again. He climbs the steps again.

A voice from the wall repeats and repeats, a soft persuasive voice: *Imagine anything. Yes, we can imagine anything. . . . Imagine anything. Yes, we can imagine anything.*

Mum screams again, clamps her hands over her ears again. She leaves.

Imagine anything. Yes, we can imagine anything. . . .

Dad laughs, shakes his head.

"That's what I say, isn't it?" he says.

"And it's true," I say.

The victim drops again.

"Tell you what else I say," says Dad. "If you can imagine doing something, then you can do it."

We turn to leave the room.

Gotcha! snaps Nattrass.

We go out again into the city streets.

"I feel . . . *defiled*," says Mum.

Dad takes her hand.

"What about loveliness?" says Mum. "What about beauty? Where's the stuff that'll touch the heart?"

3

The tent's blue canvas. It's down by the fire pit. I sleep in it night after night. I light fires in the pit. I put up a little camping table and a camping stool. I light a camping gaz lamp and I read down there. I keep my knife Death Dealer with me. I look at the stars. I wait for Crystal and Oliver. I know they'll come. I'll be ready for them.

When I was small, when I first started sleeping out, Mum asked me, "Will you not get scared?"

"Of what?" I asked.

Dad raised his hands like claws and rolled his eyes.

"Of monsters, lad!" he hissed. "Of goblins and werewolves and ghoulies and ghosts!"

He mimed biting a child's head off.

I mimed wringing my own neck. Bared my teeth like fangs.

"Course I'm not scared," I said.

Mum shrugged.

"I'll leave the door open in case you want to come back in."

I never once went back. I was scared, though. That was part of the joy of it. Max and I told each other tales about the fiends and ghosts that roamed Northumberland: white ladies, horned devils, headless horsemen, gray children. We invented Farmer Flynn, who prowled the village gardens with a hatchet in his hand and murder in his heart. He looked for kids, especially for kids whose parents let them sleep outside in tents. He reached in through tent doorways. He slid his hands under groundsheets. He caught the sleeping children with his claw-like fingers. He dragged them to his abattoir, where he laughed as he chopped them and sawed them and bled them and minced them and handed them to his wife, Plump Betty. She mixed the children's flesh with spices and herbs. She boiled them up on her ancient Aga. She baked them, turned them into pies and pates and sausages to sell at the county fair and village fetes and village shops.

"Oh, here he comes," we'd whisper in the deep dead dark of three a.m. "He's creeping nearer. I can hear his breath. Oh no, he's almost here. Oh no, he's at the door! No, I don't want to be turned into sausages, Farmer Flynn! No! No! Aaaaaaagh!"

I dream of Farmer Flynn. I dream of Crystal and Oliver, of Nattrass and knives and Spotlight and snakes.

One night Mum brings some hot chocolate down for me, like she used to.

"No Max these days?" she says.

"He's getting too old for sleeping out," I say. "Boring and old."

"Or maybe he's moved to other things. Like girls, for instance."

She smiles. I shrug.

"Maybe," I say.

I think of Becky and Kim. I think of Crystal, of her green eyes, her pale skin, her kiss on my cheek.

"Summer'll soon be gone," I say.

"Most years it'd have been gone already."

"I want to do more."

"More?"

"Before the summer's gone. I want to take my sleeping bag, a bit of food. I want to sleep out in the open. Just for a night or two."

She laughs at me.

"What a boy," she says.

"There couldn't be anywhere safer to do it," I say. "And it's still warm enough, and—"

"And by the time next year comes round you might have moved on to other things."

"Yes."

She regards me.

"We couldn't let you do something like that. Could we?"

"Nothing'll happen. It'll be something to remember for the rest of my life."

I look at her.

"You know it's the kind of thing you want for me. You don't want me boring and tame. Let me do it."

"I'll have to talk it through with Dad."

And I know what he'll say:

Live an adventure. Live like you're in a story.

4

That night I try to clear my mind of everything but Crystal and Oliver. I try to draw them to me by the power of thought. I imagine their journey. They move out of the city into the emptiness beyond. They walk on country lanes, on boggy footpaths. They're tiny figures in the hugeness of Northumberland. I see them hiding in sheds and ditches by day. I see them stealing fruit from country gardens, catching rabbits, gulping icy water from streams. The dream deepens, strengthens. I rise from the floor of the tent. I look down and see myself lying there, brown, long-haired, eyes closed. I move higher, through the blue canvas, into the air outside. I look down upon my tent, my flickering fire, my house. I see Dad behind his window, his face illuminated by the glow of his computer screen. A great silver moon has risen over the moors, and the countryside's bathed in its silvery light. Bats flicker around me. There are owls. I see the orange glow of the city in the distant sky. I see the village streetlights, the lights in houses and cottages. I move eastwards. I see the silver slick of the river, the dark ribbons of the military road and the wall. I see the great dark emptiness to the north. It's dreaming but not like dreaming. It's like moving weightlessly, easily, comfortably. I pause over the ridge, over St. Michael and All Angels. I look down upon the surface of the world and it's beautiful under the moon, and I see how it is like Mum's photographs, how it is like skin. And I move to the east again and follow the route of the wall, the thing that once marked the division between wildness and civilization. And I see them, the two figures, striding loosely and easily. They move through the field beside the wall. Their moon shadows fall before them. I want to fall, to swoop down, to descend from my dream to their side and say, *Here you are at last! Here I am!* But suddenly I'm awake again and lying alone in my tent. I try to sleep again, to return to my dream of flight, but when sleep does come it's empty, nothing but restless shadows.

5

Next morning, though, it's like the dream continues, like it's all around me. I go up to the house through the brilliant morning light. Mum's gone off to Newcastle. I sip some juice. I look out the back window towards the sheep and cows and grass and the blazing sun.

I hear Dad moving about upstairs. I hear his printer. Soon he's on the stairs and coming into the kitchen. He looks at the clock.

"No school?" he says.

I look straight back at him.

"Thought I might stay off," I say. "I'm . . ."

I think about finding an excuse, but I just shrug.

"Young," he says.

"Yes," I say. "I'm young."

And he shrugs, too.

He puts the kettle on, spoons coffee into a cup.

"Thomas Fell," he says.

"Eh?"

"Thomas Fell. Remember? They found his body in the hills."

"The German. The old prisoner of war. The tramp."

"The *wanderer* is a better description. But yes, that's him."

"What about him?"

He grins. He clenches his fists. He bites his lip.

"He's the father, Liam," he says.

"What?"

"He's the father of the foundling."

"Of Alison?"

"Yes!"

I rub my eyes. Am I still asleep? Dad watches me and grins.

"But he was eighty years old," I say.

"Doesn't matter. It's possible. He was the father; the woman in the red hat, who is a troubled young woman from the northern fells, is the mother. It was his final affair, perhaps his only ever affair, right at the end of his lonely life. Then he died, and in her grief and confusion, the mother left their baby to be discovered in Rook Hall."

"Have you tried this out on Mum?"

"You know I don't tell anybody my stories when I'm only halfway through."

"You're telling me."

"But you're involved in it. You're the one that found the foundling. Anyway, she'd probably say it was barmy."

"It *is* barmy."

"Maybe. But it's a great story."

I start asking more, but he shakes his head, puts his finger to his lips.

"No! Too much talk'll put a stop to it."

I sigh, shake my head. He laughs.

"By the way," he says. "Mum told me about your own romantic notion. Your desire for a bit of wandering nighttime vagabondage." He grins. "Looks like barminess runs in the family, eh? You reckon you'll be safe?"

"Course I will."

"Sounds fine to me. Wish I'd had a chance when I was a kid."

He stares out the window with me. A distant black jet streaks over Hallington Ridge.

"Thomas Fell," he murmurs. "Prisoner of war. Treasure collector. Foundling father. It all fits."

He puts his hand on my shoulder.

"Sometimes it's like dreaming," he says. "It's like having visions. You see the story, you see the characters, you hear their voices. The story goes on, takes its own shape, like it's destined to be that way." His eyes glaze over. He laughs. "Anyway, you do your romantic wandering. I'll put my bum on a boring seat and write the words."

"OK."

He goes away again.

I stay by the tent all day. I read, I play with fires, I sharpen Death Dealer.

6

Late afternoon I go to Max's.

"Where you been?" he says.

"I've been desperately ill."

"Ill! Your parents are too soft, that's your trouble."

"Bet I didn't miss much."

He counts the topics off on his fingers.

"Write a poem about spring. Trigonometry. Are people born good or bad or does environment make them that way? The origins of the First World War. And dead cow and dumplings with lumpy rutabega."

"See?"

We're in his bedroom. He's got his homework spread on his desk in front of him. Posters of Che Guevara, Wayne Rooney and a Massey Ferguson tractor are on his wall.

I lower my voice.

"Oliver and Crystal are on their way," I say. "I'm sure of it."

"Oh aye?"

"Aye. So I thought we should take them up to Kane's Cave."

"Kane's Cave?"

"You know. One of the places we stashed all that stuff."

"What stuff?"

"Hell's teeth, Max. The food and everything. When we were kids. For when the war or the plague comes. *Remember?*"

He shakes his head.

"God, we were really into it, eh? All that war and stupid surviving stuff."

"And it worked, didn't it? We've got provisions, we've got a place to hide them from the world."

He groans.

"So the last days are about to start, are they? The end of the world is nigh! Grow up, man, Liam."

"And you grow down, you boring git. Mr. Agricultural Engineer. Mr. Nice Little Northumbrian Girlfriend Kim."

"Shove off, poser."

"Is that what I am?"

He shoves his homework aside. He grits his teeth and stands up.

"Yes you are," he says. "You and your asylum seeker. What's he got to do with you?"

"So he's nothing to do with us. So we wash our hands of him? So we let them send him back to—"

"What do you know about it? What do you know about

Liberia and slaughter? You're an innocent, Liam. What you going to do when he turns on *you*?"

"Huh! What do you mean, turns on me?"

"What I mean is you're playing with fire."

We're inches apart, glaring.

"Anyway," he says. "It's not *him*, is it?"

"Eh?"

"It's *her*. It's that punky little lass, isn't it. She's the—"

I grab his collar. He just grins.

"I'm right, aren't I?" he says.

"She's not Becky sweet little Smith, if that's what you mean! She's not Kim little—"

He grabs my throat, knees me in the groin, shoves me down, holds me down. His face is right over mine.

"This is how tough you are, Liam," he whispers. "You're a birk. You're a stupid innocent birk. . . ."

I reach down. I get out Death Dealer. I hold it up in front of him.

"Oh no!" he laughs. "It's Liam Lynch and his pruning knife!"

He grabs my wrist. He forces the knife back towards me.

"Don't you threaten me," he snarls.

Then there's footsteps on the stairs, Max's dad's voice.

"Max! You lads OK in there?"

We get up, straighten our clothes. I shove the knife back into the sheath.

"Aye!" calls Max.

There's a knock at the door. It opens. His dad's there.

"All right, lads?" he says.

"Aye," we say.

"All right, Liam?"

"Aye."

He comes closer. There's tears in my eyes.

"You sure now, son?"

"Aye," I say again.

"Good." He reaches out and straightens Max's collar. "Max's got a lot on, son," he says.

"Yes. I know."

"You weren't at school today, I hear."

"No."

"Not well?"

"No."

"You look fit enough to me, son." His face hardens. I see the look in his eyes. I'm a bad influence. I'm a weirdo from a weird family. "I wouldn't like to think you were stopping our Max getting on," he says.

"I'm not," I tell him.

"Mebbe it's best you get back to your own work, then."

I move towards the door. He opens it wide so I can get through.

"We just get one chance at life," he says.

"I *know* that," I tell him.

"Then you'll know we've got to make the most of it, haven't we?"

"I know *that*, as well."

"Good. You go home and do your homework, then, and get a good night's sleep. You'll see Max on the bus tomorrow. If your condition improves, that is."

I shove past him. I go out.

The night's dead still. The sky's orange, yellow, red as fire. I head homewards.

A voice hisses from the shadows.

"So. What did you *think?*"

7

He steps out. He reaches towards me. He grabs my a[r]
me back.

"I said, What did you *think*?"

Nattrass, of course.

"I know you went," he says. "I had me spies out.
thought that Gordon Nattrass'd turn out be an artist

I try to pull away. He grips me tighter.

"We've got a title for it all now," he says. "Shoul[d]
from the start it's so obvious. *The Human Beast*, we
it. What d'you *think*?"

I stop moving, I let him grip me, I let him talk.
be done.

"But doesn't matter what *you* think, Liam. *The*[y]
great. *They* want me to do more. *They* think I'm so

arty savage and they've never come across nowt like me comes in close. He whispers in my ear. "They give me with all the stuff like sound effects and complicated tec stuff. But it's *mine*, Liam. That's what they say. It's my work It's my *vision*."

He laughs.

"I am a visionary artist, Liam."

I wait. He keeps on laughing. His breath is on my face.

"So have they arrived yet?" he says.

"What?"

"Have they *arrived*?"

He grins.

"Now, that got you, didn't it?"

I stop struggling. I have to know what he knows.

"Like I said, I've got me spies out," he says. "And there's talk of a black lad and a white lass walking in Northumberland. A black lad and a white lass that look like they should be some-where else, certainly not on country lanes, and they stick out by a mile. So who on earth could they be, I wonder. And where would they be heading for? It's a mystery, eh? Or mebbe it isn't a mystery at all."

He licks his lips.

"Not saying nothing, brother?" he whispers. "Cat got your tongue, brother?"

I turn my eyes from him. I see him lying on the earth with my knife in him. I blink away the vision and I move at last. His laughter follows, follows.

8

Mum's in the kitchen when I get back. There's a big sheet of wallpaper rolled out on the table. She's daubing Alison's hands with paints, helping her to make handprints, helping her to smear hand trails and finger trails of paint.

"This one should long be in bed," she says. "But we painted and painted and painted and . . ."

She shows me a great ring of green and blue paint on the paper. "This is me. Isn't it, Alison?"

Alison giggles and gurgles and daubs some more.

"And now it's Liam's turn," says Mum.

She unrolls a stretch of clean paper.

"Tell him to stand still," says Mum.

Alison gurgles.

"What color?" says Mum.

Alison plunges her fist into a pot of black. She drags it across the paper. She swipes yellow over it, green, orange, red. She giggles. There's paint all over her face and arms, all over the table, dripping to the floor.

"Let's do his eyes," says Mum. "Let's do his mouth. Let's make him really really horrible!"

She holds Alison's hands, pats them down to make weird facial features. They giggle together. Mum holds the painting up. It's a weird goggly-eyed thing with yellow hair bursting out all around the head. The paint slithers and runs and drips off the page.

"This is your Liam!" Mum says. "Look at him. He's a monster!"

Alison laughs and laughs. There's paint on her face, on her lips, on her tongue.

"O-A!" she echoes, trying to talk. "O-A O-A O-A!"

I make wild faces. I take a fingertip of red paint and make jagged marks on my face. Alison laughs and screams.

"Aaaagh!" cries Mum.

"Aaaaaaagh!" cries Alison.

"Run!" says Mum. "Liam is a monster!"

She picks the baby up.

"Come on," she says. "Let's get away. Where shall we go? I know! The bath!"

And they're gone, and Dad comes in.

"Still with us?" he says.

"More visions?" I say.

"Yes," we both answer.

9

I light my fire. I eat slices of cold pizza and drink lemonade. I have Death Dealer. I have the money from Alison's jar. I read at the little table by the camping gaz light. I watch the moon rise over Northumberland. I peer into the dark. I listen. I look back to the house and see Dad looking towards me from his window. I wave. Can he see me? He waves and turns back to his work. The moon climbs higher. I see the silhouette of St. Michael and All Angels against the eastern sky. I throw more sticks onto the fire and it flares and scatters sparks like dancing stars. I try to stay awake but I keep slumping in my chair, keep drifting. I hear the baby crying. I hear Nattrass's voice and the dreadful noises of his exhibition. I hear Dad's fingers on his computer keys and the whirring of his printer. I hear owls, and distant barks and howls and screeches. I hear my heart, its steady beat, the crackle of flames, the hiss of embers. Voices speak inside me. Mum: *I'm not meat! It isn't in me!* Alison: *O-A! O-A! O-A!* And Crystal's voice. Then silence and deep darkness until I find myself rising again and looking back down upon myself, slumped in the chair by my fire. I rise into the moonlit night. I look down upon the house, my tent, my fire, my village. There's the wall, the road, the distant orange glow of the city. The earth is beautiful. Silvery light, dark shadows, a multitude of sheep, lights glowing in cottages, the headlights of a few cars, stars and stars and darkness deep around them and beyond them. The great dark rolling horizons to the north. I pause over the ridge above the village, above the chapel of St. Michael and All Angels. And there they are, two figures moving through the field towards the chapel. I want to call out their names, to tell them I'm here. I drop lower. I can hear their feet moving through the dry grass. I hear the click of the latch as they open the little gate, hear the creak as they pull the gate open. They enter the garden of gravestones around the chapel. The sheep that are lying there shift in their sleep. The two figures move towards the further wall of the churchyard. They point down towards the village. They point towards a tiny distant flickering light. I hear the murmur of their voices. I can make out one word: *Liam*. I try to call out to them, but have no voice. I want to go lower but I can't. I have no control of what I do. I watch them hold each other. They become one shape, one shadow. Then they separate, pass through a stile in the wall. They move downhill towards the village through the fields.

Then the vision's gone, and I'm in a deep empty dreamless sleep, then I'm awake and slumped in the chair by the fire, and filled with the vision of having been out there, up there. I keep my eyes closed, wanting the vision to linger.

Then there are footsteps in the garden. And a voice.

"Liam! Liam!"

Crystal's voice.

10

They come from the shadows under the trees, like figures from a dream. I see the gleam of Oliver's face, the white bloom of Crystal's. They move across the grass towards me. I grunt a greeting. Can hardly speak. Crystal kisses my cheek. I don't know what to do. They have little rucksacks, with sleeping bags attached to them. They pull them off. I tremble. I don't know what to say.

"The police came," I mutter.

"Of course they did," says Crystal. "We're escapees, runaways, fugitives."

"Where will you go?"

"Where they won't find us," says Oliver.

"The back of beyond," says Crystal. "And then beyond that." She laughs. "Can you point us in the right direction, Liam?"

I just stare. Crystal waves her hand before my eyes. Her pale cheeks, her green eyes, her grin.

"He thinks we're a dream, Ollie. Wake up, Liam." She takes my hand, touches her cheek with it. "We're real," she says. "We're here in your tent. And mebbe we could hide in it forever and forever, but mebbe not."

"Were you at the chapel?" I ask.

"The place where Alison was christened?" says Crystal.

"Aye."

"We were," says Crystal. "We were heading for you, Liam. Liam'll help us, we said. We came to the chapel and we looked down and we saw your fire flickering. That'll be him, we said. It'll be his sign. He'll be watching, he'll be waiting. Were you?"

"Yes," I say. "Yes. As soon as I heard you'd gone, I knew you'd come."

"I knew you'd know." She holds my shoulders. She looks into my eyes. "We couldn't not have come. It's fate, Liam."

"Yes," I say. "It's fate."

She grins.

"Wake up," she says.

"Wake up," says Oliver.

They're both laughing.

"It's so exciting," says Crystal. "Running off, heading out of the city. All the darkness outside, all the light and all the space. We slept the first night in a graveyard. The next in somebody's shed, till a dog starts barking and chases us away. Then bus shelters and barns and oh so many places . . ."

"Lettuces from people's gardens," says Oliver. "And carrots and—"

"You had no money?" I say.

"Just a little," says Oliver. "We have to look after it. We might be gone a long time."

"Last night we ate a chicken," says Crystal. "Oliver killed it with his knife. We cooked it on a fire, the poor little thing. It was absolutely lovely. We buried its bones. We thanked it for being our prey. We wished its spirit safe passage into the dark."

I get out some food: cheese, bread, biscuits, stuff I brought out from the house. They eat it ravenously.

"I have some money you can have, as well," I say.

"You're a good person, Liam," says Oliver. "Don't do anything you might regret."

"I won't," I say.

I lick my lips. I hesitate.

"I'd like to come with you," I say.

Crystal laughs.

"To the back of beyond?" she says.

"Yes." I laugh as well. "Just for a little while. I know the way."

"Then perhaps you should," she says. "What do you think, Ol?"

He lifts his shoulders slowly.

"Maybe you should, Liam. But you must take great care."

Outside, the sky's already starting to get light.

"We should move," I say.

11

I roll up my sleeping bag. I strap Death Dealer to my belt. I slip into the house, collect bread, fruit, cheese, sausages, ham, put it into a rucksack. I write a little note: *Gone wandering. Back soon-ish. xL.* I hang the note on the tent door, then I lead Crystal and Oliver out of the garden and into the fields through the predawn light. I lead them around the edges of growing crops. I open and close gates. I retrace the route towards Alison's finding place. The light intensifies, a low mist blankets the river, skylarks sing and curlews call. The air's cool and bright. We walk. I imagine walking with Oliver and Crystal into the back of beyond and beyond, disappearing from my old life, beginning again, being born again.

Jak jak!

It's there in front of us, perching on a gate. It flaps its wings. It bobs.

Jak jak!

"A crow!" says Crystal.

"A raven, townie," I say, and smile.

"Jak jak!" I cry. "Hello there, Jack!"

We come to Rook Hall. We clamber inside, totter on the fallen stones. The sun rises, a great orange ball in the eastern sky. Its light pours in through Rook Hall's gaping roof, shines through chinks and gaps in the walls. A raven perches on the broken wall above.

Jak jak! Jak jak!

We sit on the ancient carved stones. We eat and drink. The mist dissolves. The river glitters and glints. Upriver, the castle turrets sharpen against the clear sky. A distant low-flying jet streaks through the sky. Then another, then another.

We trace the patterns of ancient rock art with our fingers. I tell them how ancient it is, how nobody knows what it means.

"Maybe it means nothing," says Crystal. "Maybe it's just itself, carvings, nice shapes and patterns in the rock."

I take out Death Dealer. I scrape the rock with its point, but I hardly make a mark. I scrape a simple pattern, a loose spiral, like a snake.

"It stands for the people who made it," says Oliver. "It says, Here I am. Here I was, before I was taken."

"Taken?" I ask.

"Taken by war, by enemies, by death. It's like when I write my tale. We're here for a while, we make our mark, and then we're taken. We're gone."

Jak jak! Jak jak!

Crystal stands up. She spreads her arms like wings. She juts her head out. She jabs the air. She calls, "Jak jak! Jak jak! Here I am! Look! I'm the raven! I stand for nothing but myself! And I am absolutely gorgeous!"

Jak jak! calls the bird.

"Jak jak!" calls Crystal. "Jak jak! Jak jak! Jak jak!"

She starts to take off her shoes.

12

She tiptoes barefooted to the river. Rolls her jeans up. Steps across the dried-out sandy bank, steps into the water and giggles at the cold. Stands shin-deep and watches the water flow smoothly across her calves. Dips her fingers in then scatters water droplets all around her head. Holds her arms out wide and turns her face to the sky and reaches up like she's about to fly. She cries the raven's call, then just calls out, part laughter, part howl, which turns to:

"I am *Crystal*! I! Am! Crystal! I am here! I am *free!*"

She wades back out again. Waves at us. She takes off her jeans, her jacket, her fleece, her T-shirt. She's so thin, so pale, so vulnerable, so beautiful and bold. She steps back into the water in her bra and pants. There are dark scars at her shoulder blades, like remnants of great wounds. She wades out until she's waist-deep. Crouches down and hoots at the cold and crouches again and wades a little deeper. She closes her eyes and plunges right in and bursts back up.

"Come *on*!" she calls. "It's *great*!"

We strip to our underwear and wade into the water. The water's icy, the riverbed's all pebbles and stones. We kick and splash and pour handfuls of water across each other. We dive and let the current carry us, we swim against the current, we swim across the river towards the other side. When we're all swum out, we stand and hug each other. Our skin is cold. Our hot hearts beat fiercely underneath.

By now Crystal's pale makeup is washed away. Her face is exposed. She puts her fingers up to the marks there, to where the skin below her left eye is red and blemished from her childhood burns. She shrugs.

"It's skin, that's all," she says. "Usually I cover it up, but sometimes I think, What the hell. . . ."

We wade out again. We stretch out in the sun on the rock beside Rook Hall. Birds sing and the river flows and the breeze whispers in the trees. A jet roars over and another jet but we just laugh and wave our fists at them.

"Just go away!" says Crystal. "Just go home and be quiet for a while."

Her razor scars are high up on her arms. The scars of her burns are on her waist and thighs. The knife scar is on Oliver's face. There are others on his chest. They're so damaged, the two of them. Crystal leans across and kisses Oliver, and I see that the scars at her shoulder blades aren't scars at all, but are black and blue and red tattoos of scars.

She sees me looking.

"My pal did them," she says. "Another foster home, couple of years back. She said I was a wounded angel."

Then Oliver sits up and looks back towards the village.

"What?" I whisper.

I look where he looks and there's nothing: empty fields, empty tracks, hedgerows. A tractor rattles in a distant field somewhere.

"Perhaps nothing," he says. "But we should go on, Liam."

And so we get dressed. I lead them on to the ancient reivers' track beside the river. We walk quickly in single file through the dappled shadows. We walk northwards, towards the place of safety that Max Woods and I prepared, long ago when we were little children.

13

It's easy at first, but soon the path's tangled and overgrown and we have to shoulder our way through dense shrubs, duck under overhanging branches. We hear dogs barking, children playing in the gardens of old estate houses. We keep low. We keep silent. The path follows the river, then curves away, then curves back again to a wide turn in the river. The bank here is a beach of great stones that clunk and slide as we tread across them. Trees have toppled here, their roots washed out by water. There are massive rocks spread out across the river. It's the ancient raiders' crossing place. On the other side, an apparently unscaleable wall of moss-covered rock. I roll up my jeans and step from rock to rock across the gushing water, and lead the others across to it, to the fissure that Max and I discovered ages back. At some time someone has cut deep footholds into

it. You climb by stepping upwards, by gripping the stems of stunted trees that grow out from the rock. And it's suprisingly easy. The fissure's wide as a man. The footholds are deep. The trees are strong. You could carry a rustled sheep on your back. You could carry the bloody body of a victim. Or you could haul them up from the top on ropes.

We hesitate at the top. We look back to the tree-lined shining river, to the castles, to the smoke rising from cottage chimneys, towards the hidden village and the city far beyond. Then we turn to the next horizon: tough grass, peaty earth, outcrops of black rock, and bleak moorland going on forever.

We walk to the north again. I think of the savage ancestors that walked here long before. Their blood and bones are mingled in the earth. Their breath is in the breeze. Their cries are in the cry of the curlew and the skylark's song. Their ancient instincts are in us. They live on in our memories, stories, dreams.

The world looks bleak. Nowhere to shelter, nowhere to hide. But I lead my friends over a ridge and there it is. A small hidden valley. There's a copse of twisted trees. There's a trickling stream, a track of stones, gorse and heather, gnarled blackthorn and hawthorn and birch, and a wall of rock behind. I lead them across the grass, into the trees, towards the rock, to the head-high cave at the heart.

14

The air's almost still. There's the gentle sound of trickling water. The cave isn't deep. A few strides and you're at the back. Must have been carved out hundreds of years ago, hammered out by raiders. I imagine them gathered here, bristling with arms, boasting about their battles, their cruelty, their wounds. I imagine their tethered stolen sheep, their sacks of plunder.

"It's Kane's Cave," I say. "One of the places we said we'd come to if a war started. Or if the world dried up or started to burn. Or if our families died in a plague."

I laugh at the daftness of children's dreams, at the beauty of them.

"Watch this," I say.

I kneel down at a moss-covered rock. It's as broad as my chest. I grip it, start to lift it. I lift the edge free of the earth. I tip it over. I scrape away the stones and soil beneath, and there it is.

"Treasure!" gasps Crystal.

A white plastic box, a foot long and nine inches deep. I pull it out. I lever the lid away with my fingertips. I lift the contents out: tins of beans and Irish stew and hot dogs; bags of boiled sweets; packets of rice and spaghetti; a chunk of Christmas cake wrapped in foil; a cigarette lighter; a pair of knives and forks; a tin opener; a compass; a sharpened pencil; a hard-backed school exercise book with a title already carefully written in my childish hand: *A Journal of the Last Days by Liam Lynch.*

Crystal giggles.

"*A Journal of the Last Days by Liam Lynch!* Liam, what a romantic!"

Everything's survived. A few blemishes, a bit of rust, that's all.

"It's a time capsule," she says. "How long's it been here?"

I shake my head.

"Four years, five years." I laugh. "We used to say that if we never needed it ourselves, then some kids or some archaeologist from years in the future would find it and know all about us. Look."

I show them the words written inside the lid of the box in black marker.

These things were placed here in the year 20— by Liam Lynch and Max Woods. We send our greetings to the people of the future.

I remember how we put it into the earth beneath the stone, how we knelt together and prayed for our families, for the people of the future and for the peace of the world. I remember how we clenched our fists after we rolled the stone back, how we promised we'd be friends forever, how we'd protect each other always, how we'd never part.

"Irish stew!" says Crystal. "Midget gems! You're a genius, Liam Lynch!"

I'm already scanning the ground again, trying to remember the other hiding place.

I stab the earth with Death Dealer. The point hits metal. I rip the turf away, shove the earth aside, and pull out a pair of aluminum cooking pots nestled into each other. I pull them apart. A pair of blue plastic bionoculars and a couple of small penknives fall out. I tug one of the knives open. It breaks, the blade snaps off and falls into the grass. I open the other one. It breaks as well.

Crystal giggles. She looks through the binoculars. She giggles more.

"What the hell did you think you'd ever see through these?"

I remember them so well. They were in my Christmas stocking along with a chocolate snowman and a book of knock-knock jokes.

"We thought we'd see the end of the world!" I say. "We thought we'd see the Third World War!"

"Oh, Liam! You must have been so *gorgeous*. Is there any *more*?"

I scan the earth. I scratch my head.

"Don't think so."

"Just you, eh? Just you and yourself as a little boy?"

She wets her finger, rubs the label on the hot dog tin.

"Yum yum. Just three years out of date."

Oliver has the notebook in his hands. It's stiff and dry. It crackles as he open it. It's empty.

"It's a lovely English story," he says. "Like Robin Hood and his merry men in the forest. King Arthur's knights riding through the wilderness. You must have had a lovely time, playing here with Max."

"Yes. We did."

I see us, lying in the long grass above the cave. We had sticks for rifles. We peered along them towards the soldiers playing war games far off to the north.

"Kapow!" we used to go. "Kapow! Kapow! Kapow!"

We lobbed stones as grenades.

"Kaboom! Kaboom!"

"We'll fight to the death!" we used to cry. "Ratatatatat! Kapow! Kaboom! Liam and Max forever!"

A jet streaks over us. We hear a dull explosion in the north. We hear the *pop pop pop* of guns.

"Just games," I say. "They won't come closer. We're just kids. We're no interest to them."

Oliver unpacks his rucksack: a few spare clothes, a long carving knife. He lays his sleeping bag out inside the cave.

We sit on stones. We look at the landscape and each other and the sky.

"You found a good spot," says Oliver.

"The perfect little spot," says Crystal.

"The perfect place for writing in," says Oliver.

We hear guns again. He pulls out his notebook. He flicks through it: page after page of black jagged words.

"You want to read it, don't you, Liam?" he says. "But

there's nothing. Lots of words and lots of nothing. The pages may as well be as empty as yours."

He puts his pen in his fist. He drags the tip across a series of finished pages, canceling them out. He turns to a new page. And he turns his attention from us, just as Dad turns his attention as he begins to write. His eyes cloud over. He rests the pen on the page and writes.

I write the date on my own first page with the old pencil. I write a few tentative lines.

I'm fourteen years old now. I'm with Crystal and Oliver. There's no plague. No war.

Oliver grunts. He bares his teeth. Suddenly he stabs the carving knife into the earth at his side. He cancels what he's written. He starts again. He glares when he sees me watching.

Crystal laughs. She's looking through the useless blue binoculars again.

"Come on," she says. "Take me for a walk, Liam."

15

We go to the head of the valley. We take some bread and ap-
ples. We sit on an outcrop of rock and eat. She takes the knife
from the sheath at my hip. She scrapes the rock with it, loops
and whirls and snaky shapes. I watch the tip of the knife
move across the surface. I'm nervous about asking what I
want to ask.

"Why do you cut yourself?" I say.

"What?"

"Is it to prove to yourself that you exist or something? Or
to punish yourself or something?" I look away. "It doesn't
matter. It's nothing to do with me."

"I don't mind. It's just a stupid thing. First time it was just
a little daft thing with a potato peeler. One Sunday lunchtime I
get bored. I'm peeling potatoes and I lift my sleeve and put the

blade of the peeler on my skin and tug. Ouch. Pain. But I don't stop. Soon it's razors and knives."

My eyes widen.

"Don't look like that," she says. "There's nothing special about it. Lots of kids in care do it. You've never wanted to, have you? Kids like you don't."

"Kids like me?"

She clicks her tongue.

"Don't be thick, Liam. You know what I mean. It must be dead boring being loved and looked after." She smiles. "Kids like you imagine being kids like me, but kids like me want nothing more than to be kids like you."

She jumps up onto the rock. She poses there and her skinny shape and wild hair are silhouetted against the brilliant sky.

"I'm weird and dramatic!" she says. "I'm a wild girl!" She steps down. "And I just wish I was one of the boring little village girls you probably turn your nose up at."

She grabs my hand, tugs me forward, and we walk across the moor.

"I'll tell you about Clarrie Dowd," she says. "I'll tell you how far kids like me'll go to imagine having other lives."

She leads me to another rock. It's covered in lichen and moss. We sit down on the grass. We lean back against the rock. I turn my face to the sun, already high up in the sky. From down in the valley we hear a sudden yell from Oliver, then another, a writer's yell, just like my dad's.

"His story's not working," I say. "He can't get it right."

"He will," says Crystal.

Then there's silence.

"Clarrie Dowd," says Crystal. "Now, there's a weird girl. We shared a home together, me and her and a few other lovely waifs and strays. It was on the seafront at Cullercoats, a lovely big stone place with lovely house parents. Clarrie used to hypnotize. We used to get together after midnight on her bed, hunched up in our pajamas with our teddy bears in our arms. She did this thing with her hands and her voice. *You are in my power. Close your eyes. Go back and back. Remember. Rememberrrr.* She took us wherever we wanted to go. She told us she believed in reincarnation. She said that all of us had lives before, in other places, other times, other bodies. She said she could lead us back to those lives. We could live in them again, if only for a short time."

"Do *you* believe that?"

"Doesn't matter what I believe. I know what I saw, sitting there on Clarrie Dowd's bed. I saw kids being lifted away from what they were. One lad remembered being a gunner in the war. He was in a gun turret in a bomber flying over Germany. *Enemies at two o'clock!* he gasped. He held the air like it was a machine gun. He stared at the ceiling like it had a flight of fighter planes in it. *Ratatatat!* he went, and the bed bounced and bounced as he fired. *Ratatatatat! Die! Die!* There was podgy little Jo Scoular. She was a maid in a grand house. Such a giggle. *Thank you, ma'am,* she used to say. *Of course, sir. Let me take your hat and coat, sir.* And some were even animals— we had a dog and a cat and even a raccoon. Imagine that, eh? Ha, and all the barking and the growling and meowing. Was like a zoo some nights."

She laughs, remembering.

"Sometimes their eyes were wide open, sometimes shut

dead tight. We couldn't wake anybody up, that was the rule. Or they might die, or be caught in some kind of limbo place. It had to be Clarrie that brought them back, Clarrie that guided them back to the room, to the bed, to their ordinary life in the home on the seafront at Cullercoats."

"Did they remember when they woke up?" I ask.

"Yeah, they did. And most of them believed that what had happened was true. It was that real, they used to say. It was like being there at that time. It was like being that person. Ha, or that cat. When they talked about it, it was like they were in a dream, or having visions. Ha. I remember one kid. There's grins all over his face. *Oh, Clarrie!* he goes. *It's just lovely being a sheep!* And we all loved her, lovely Clarrie Dowd. She was some kind of a saint. I'm sure she was." She pauses. "This is so weird, telling it all like this. Never told it all before. It must be something about being out here in the open."

"And what about you?"

"Me?"

"What did Clarrie do to you?"

"I didn't want to do it, not for a long long time. And Clarrie never pressed none of us to it. She said it must be us that made the decision or it could go all wrong. I think I was scared of the fire, of finding myself in it again. I told Clarrie that and she said that yes, I might have to go through the fire, but I could go further back, to the time before the fire if I wanted to. She was so sweet. She was a bit older than us all. Her poor mum had been a drug death. Her rotten dad was long long gone. She said she sometimes slipped automatically into her own past lives and there were dozens of them. She said the best lives were the lives lived on water. She said she'd been a cook on the *Queen Mary*. She'd been a pirate called Dirty Dot with a wicked cat called Pete. She said she had glimpses of a life lived long long long ago when she was without legs. She had a tail. She lived in a beautiful blue lagoon with blue and yellow fish and an octopus and she was a mermaid, and that, she said, looked like the happiest of all times for her. Did she believe it all? She said she did. And she was happy and kind and we loved the power she had on us and the power she gave to us. And it was something else to be on the bed together with the beauty and the mystery of other lives around us."

She keeps on scraping with the knife. She makes two joined curved shapes, like wings. She carves them deeper.

"My mark," she says. "The phoenix." She scrapes again, below the wings. "And look, these are the flames."

"And did you go back to the time before the fire?" I say.

"In the end I did. I remember going through the flames themselves and it was terrifying. But Clarrie guided me back, back. And I saw them, my mam and dad and the ones that were lost and I felt their touch on me and their breath on me. And I believed it, too, and when I came back to the bed I remembered it so clear, and I was so pleased."

She holds the knife up. She presses her thumb against the blunt tip.

"I'm ruining it," she says.

"It'll sharpen. And look, you're making proper rock art with it."

She carves again, going deeper.

"It'll be here forever," she says. "Folk in the future'll say, What on earth could it possibly mean?"

"And did you go further back?" I say.

"To other lives? No. Clarrie said did I want to but I said no. I said I wanted this life to be enough for me. So I went no further than when I was a little one in my family's arms and only went there two or three times. I was scared of wanting it too much, scared that going back might turn to some kind of drug that stopped me growing up properly in the here and now."

"And . . . ?"

But she laughs and presses her finger to my lips.

"And in the end," she says, "good Clarrie was took away from us to another home. And people come and asked about her but we told them she did only good things and she let us talk about the past. And some of us like her moved on again. That's what it is to be a kid like me. You move from one home to another home and meet many that's kind. And there's always those who have gone from our lives, and those people are like ghosts, like scattered bits of memory, like things you miss, like dreams you carry round with you."

She smiles.

"And anyway," she says, "all life sometimes seems like dreams. Do you think so, Liam?"

"Yes," I say.

"Good."

She puts the knife in my hand.

"Now it's your turn," she says. "Show me what your mark looks like."

I have no idea. I hold the point of the knife to the rock and just doodle. Then I make a spiral and that feels right, so I go round and round with the knife, spinning it to the center of the spiral and then out to the edge again. And we work like that as the day wears on, as explosions thud in the north, as distant rifles rattle, as Oliver sometimes gasps in frustration in the valley below. We pass the knife back and forward, we make our weird and beautiful marks in the stone.

16

We go back down. Oliver's still hunched up, writing. He looks at us like he's looking into a different world.

"Time for food," says Crystal. "Not midget gems and hot dogs, though."

He doesn't smile.

I light a fire. I put the sausages I brought from home into an aluminum pan. They start to sizzle and spit.

"How did the writing go?" I say to Oliver.

He rips out a page and drops it onto the fire.

"Words are too easy," he says. He opens his book. "What looks like truth and sounds like truth might be nothing but a dream, nothing but a story I wish had happened."

I stab the sausages with my knife. Fat and juice ooze out. Crystal tries to take Oliver's hand but he pulls away. He rips another page out of his book, crushes it in his fist, throws it on the flames.

"Lies," he says.

"I know how hard it is," I say.

"Do you?" says Oliver.

"Yes."

"How can you know, you with your family, here safe in Northumberland?"

"My dad," I say. "He's a writer."

"Your dad! Huh."

He turns over the pages on the fire.

"Never mind. It is best that you do not know. You're young. What's the good of knowing?"

"Knowing what?"

He turns his face to the sky and groans.

· "I should go on by myself," he says. "What's further north, Liam?"

"A few villages, a few castles, some ruins, lots of empty space, then Scotland, and more empty space."

"So I could wander in the emptiness until I die. A true refugee, all alone, left over from a distant war."

"Yes."

"No!" whispers Crystal.

He shows us a knife is in his hand.

"See how it sits there so naturally," he says.

He spins it, catches it. He stabs the earth with it.

"See?" he says again.

"Yes."

"Yes. It is at home in my hand, wherever I might be."

He spins it again. He raises it high, as if he's about to kill.

Then he leans forward towards me. He presses his thumb against the knife blade.

"I am not what you think I am," he says.

Then he's silent. I turn the sausages with the knife. The sun is lower in the sky. It'll soon be dusk. I lift out the sausages. I put them on bread. I pass a sandwich to Crystal and one to Oliver. He takes it. He eats. He rips more pages from his book. He throws them into the flames. He rips more pages, burns them, too.

"Lies," he mutters. "Lies, lies."

He stirs the fire. His eyes gleam as he stares into the gathering dark.

Crystal reaches out to him.

"Oliver!" she says.

He draws away. He laughs.

"Oliver? Who is Oliver?"

He sighs.

"Listen closely, children. I will tell you about the darkness at the heart of the world. My name is Henry Meadows. I am seventeen years old."

17

He waits a moment. He laughs again.

"Yes. I am Henry Meadows. I am seventeen years old. You will ask, But why should I believe this thing and not the other thing? I don't know why, except that this is true. So do not doubt these things. Look, I burn the lies so that what is left behind is truth. There are the ashes lying at our feet. Let me tell you about my childhood. Shall I do that? Yes? Then I remember being a boy, a pretty little ordinary boy named Henry. It was a different world, a different age. I remember my mother and my father and my sister and my brother a million miles and a million million years ago. What did we have? Nothing. A field. A hut. But I remember playing in the dust and being happy. I remember piling stones at the edge of the field while the hot sun beat down upon my back and my father sang in the field a hundred meters away. I remember my mother singing in the hut in the hot nights. I remember the skin of my young brother as we lay together sleeping. I remember the way he would kick and kick as he played football in his sleep. I remember my young sister clapping and chanting. I remember the way she would call my name. Hin-er-eee! Hin-er-eee! Hin-er-eee!"

He pauses. He repeats the words: *Hin-er-ee! Hin-er-ee!*

"I am Henry Meadows," he repeats. "I have told nobody these things since I began my journey."

He places the whole book on the fire and watches as it burns.

"My father, Joseph, was a good man. He was an optimistic man. All through his life there had been war after war after war, but he said that the world would surely change. He said that in some parts of the world all war was over and would never come again. In such places, man had seen the foolishness of his ways. He said that boys like me would find a place in this world. He said that I must see myself as a person in the world, not just a person in this village, in this country, Liberia. He said that when I had grown, I must travel. I must go to Europe, to America. Then perhaps I could come back to my homeland as an educated man, and help to make my homeland a great land. He used to laugh as he said these things to me. *Listen to me, Joseph Meadows, a man with nothing, saying these words in this poor little place, to this poor little half-naked boy. But I am right, Henry. You must learn, you must grow, you must dream, and you must leave.* And he would kiss me, and say that one day there would be a kiss to send me off for a long time. *In the meantime, you must work, you must pick stones, and you must go to school."*

He looks across the flames at me.

"Perhaps it will always be so," he says. "That fathers wish their children to live their lives for them. Is it so, Liam?"

I think of Dad: *Live like you're in a story, Liam. Live an adventure.*

"Yes," I say. "It is true."

"School was a row of benches, a blue cotton canopy, children sitting in rows a few hours each week. We scratched words on slates with sticks. Those of us without slates and sticks leaned over and wrote with our fingers in the dust. We chanted numbers and alphabets and patriotic songs. We listened to stories about our people and about the strange animals that lived around us. The teacher held up a picture of a cow and we called out 'Cow' and we wrote *cow*. A picture of a snake and we said 'Snake' and wrote down *snake*. He told us that Liberia meant 'the land of the free.' He told us it was our duty to work hard and to build a great nation of the free. He had a box in which there were faded books from long ago. When we worked hard he showed them to us. I remember how they crackled as he opened them. And I remember the pictures: New York, Californian beaches, London, Buckingham Palace, the fields of Kent, Salisbury Cathedral. These were my pictures of a world without war, and it was a world that was very beautiful to me."

The distant explosions continue. There are flashes and flares. Then pinpoints of light moving through the darkness to the north.

"I was not in the long grass when the soldiers came," he says. "I was in school. I was eight years old. It was hot. It was late afternoon. We were chanting numbers. Two add two is four, four add four is eight, eight add eight is sixteen. Just as you must have done in your school, Liam. Am I correct?"

"Yes," I say, and for a moment the chanting from my infant class comes back to me.

"We heard the guns," he says. "The *pop-pop-pop* of guns, as if from far away. Somehow they seemed not loud enough, not savage enough for guns. But there they were, and very close. We stared at each other, and at the teacher. What is it, Teacher? What is happening? What is that screaming? We said the words in innocence, but each of us knew that we had always waited for this day, when the guns and death would come to visit our little ordinary village. The popping came again, much more of it. Smoke began to rise above the far side of the village. The teacher told us to run, to hide, but too late. The soldiers were already here, in the school itself, with their guns and hatchets raised, telling us to keep silent, to sit on our benches and keep still. And there they were walking through the spaces between our homes. They fired into open doorways, they set fire to our homes with blazing torches. They looked so calm. It appeared to be so ordinary. How can I tell you about what they did to those whose lives I had shared? You would only ask, But how could they do such things, Henry? Or Oliver. Or whatever your name is."

He reaches forward and prods the burning book with a stick, making sure that each of its pages burns.

"They took your family?" I say.

"Yes, they did. As I told you. But I was not in the long grass. I was in school. And they were slaughtered, simply and calmly, like so many others were that day."

"But why?"

175

"Why? There should be a reason, yes? And it is disgusting, no? It is beyond belief. But it is not beyond belief. It happens every hour, every day. It happens as we sit here together by our fire tonight. How could people *do* such things? Oh, I would learn how they could do it, soon enough. I would soon learn how simple it is."

He pauses again. He narrows his eyes and looks towards the head of the valley. I turn to look where he looks. I listen.

"What is it?" I ask him.

"I don't know. Nothing. It doesn't matter."

We all watch and listen together. Then Oliver continues.

"Then all of them gathered at the school, and they laughed to see us there, so young, so innocent, so terrified. And our teacher told them they must go away *now*! He told them we were only *children*! And we sat on our benches and watched as they took him with a single shot."

He pauses. He looks down and waits. A voice comes from the darkness.

"Spotlight!"

And a beam of powerful light shines upon us.

18

They come through the trees. The torchlight glares on us. Nattrass holds the camera to his eye. Eddie and Ned walk at his side.

"Spotlight!" Nattrass calls again. "Spotlight spotted you in the night! You're out!"

He giggles.

"Oh, you do like your fireside chats, don't you?" he says.

"Go away, Nattrass," I sigh.

"But we're making a documentary, brother. *Everyday Life in a Northumbrian Village.* And who'd expect *this* to be going on?"

Eddie's carrying a jagged stone in his hand. A claw hammer hangs from Ned's belt.

"Here we are in the realm of the reivers and the raiders

and ancient wars," says Nattrass. "Ghosts all around us. Blood in the soil. Out here, the savage past is with us still." He laughs. "I'm good, aren't I, brother? And I'm getting better. All this art stuff's great. And you know, it's all thanks to you. I'd never have seen the possibilities if you and your family weren't in town."

He points the camera into Oliver's face.

"A few words for the viewers?" he says softly. "Don't be shy. What do you think of English country life so far, Mr. Whatdeyecallit?"

"My name is Henry," says Henry. "English country life is very good."

"Wonderful! Beautifully put! That's so good to know. And you, miss. You look like—how shall I put it?" He sniggers. "Let's say like you've seen a bit of life. So how does being in this lovely place compare with where you've been?"

"Piss off," she says.

"Oh no. Another one for the editing, lads. Never mind. The pictures are great. Here they are at home around the fire. Our fugitives: the writer's son, the black boy and the tart."

Eddie snorts with laughter.

"That's great!" he says. "The writer's son, the black boy and the tart."

"Sounds like a title, eh?" says Nattrass. "Now we need some action."

He lowers the camera. We don't move.

"I heard tell there was a black boy walking in Northumberland," he says. "Heard tell he was walking with a scrawny punk lass. So I goes, Aha! That'll be nobody else but

Liam's pals. They'll be wanting to send the lad back to his hovel and he'll be up and off and running away. Is that about the way of it? No answer, eh? Ah, well. It must be so. So I says, Law-abiding folk like me had better keep their eyes peeled, hadn't we? We don't want villains running away from the law and hiding out here on our lovely moors and refusing to get back to where they come from, do we? After all . . ." He laughs at the thought of it. "Mebbe they're terrorists. Mebbe they're war criminals. And mebbe most likely they're just liars and parasites and scum." And he kicks Oliver, lightly, with the toe of his boot. "Come on. Best if you come back with us, sunshine." He licks his lips. "Or do we think he's going to struggle, lads? It'll look great if he does, of course. The savage, turning savage." He stands over Oliver. "Come on," he says. "What you gonna do?"

I jump from my rock and go for him. I shove him down. I punch him in the face again, again. I tell him he knows nothing, he's a fascist pig. We struggle in the dirt. Then I'm kicked in the face and everything reels till I open my eyes again and Ned's kneeling over me with the hammer raised.

"You done that too many times, brother," says Nattrass. He spits snot and blood. "So mebbe I should do you now, eh? It'd be self-defense. We've got the evidence."

"Just bloody dare," says Crystal.

She raises her fists. Oliver stays sitting on his rock. Then he says,

"I was telling my story. You interrupted us."

"Oh, I ruined story time, lads! How's the diddums going to get to sleep?"

"You should go home, Nattrass," says Oliver.

Nattrass laughs.

"You should," says Oliver. "You don't want to be messing about with somebody like me."

Oliver stands up. Nattrass backs away when he sees the knife in Oliver's fist.

"I don't want any trouble," he says. His voice is shaking.

"But you're the one that brought the trouble," says Oliver. "Nobody asked you to come here, did they?"

Eddie and Ned turn away. They run back into the dark. Nattrass drops the camera. He takes out a knife of his own.

"Don't, Nattrass!" I say. "Just run!"

But suddenly Oliver has him. He holds him tight. He holds the knife at Nattrass's throat.

"I was telling my story," he whispers. "Now you have to listen, too. If you move, I'll slit your throat." He turns his eyes to me. "Keep back, Liam, or I'll slit his throat." He smiles. "Or maybe you would like me to?"

"No!" says Nattrass.

"We'll see," says Oliver. "Anyway, keep still, and I'll continue. You've missed some of the tale, Nattrass, but that should be no problem. Just imagine this. I was eight years old. There I was in an ordinary village with my ordinary friends in an ordinary little village school. The soldiers came. They slaughtered my family. They shot my teacher, and they took us all. That's where we're up to." He laughs. "They took us all. Perhaps you don't know what I mean. They took us all, and they turned us into soldiers."

"Soldiers?" says Crystal. "But you were eight years old."

He laughs.

"Crystal, the world is filled with eight-year-old soldiers.

And seven-year-olds, nine-year-olds, ten-year-olds—if they last long enough. Boys and girls." He presses the knife to Nattrass's skin. "Did you know that, Nattrass?"

"No," whispers Nattrass.

"But you *should*. And now you *do*! Do not forget it."

He touches the tiny trickle of blood that runs down the skin of Nattrass's throat.

"Oh, dear," he whispers. "I told you to keep still. It will be dangerous for you to move. Why children? Well, it is perfectly understandable. We are small. We are enthusiastic. We can be made to be obedient and brave. We want to *love*. Isn't that true, Nattrass? We want to love and to be loved. Don't we?"

"Yes," says Nattrass.

"Yes. And so if they take away our mothers and fathers and put monsters in their place and the monsters care for us and tell us what to do, then we will follow the monsters, we will love the monsters. And we will think that war is play. Because we just love to be wild. Don't we? Yes, we do. And we are unimportant and insignificant, and there are many many many of us, so it doesn't matter when we die."

Nattrass keeps dead still. His terrified eyes are on me.

"It could have been any of us," I say. "If we had been born in a different place, in a different time. It could have been me, or Crystal. . . ."

"But it was not you. It was me. They killed my family, they killed my teacher, they gave me guns, they fed me drugs. We hid out. We hunted for our food. We raided and robbed. Sometimes we were even happy. Can you believe that?" He laughs. "We were sometimes *happy*, Nattrass! Do you know what it means to be happy? We sang songs. We skipped and marched. We walked arm in arm with our companions. It was such fun. One day they will tell tales about us. When enough time has passed, we may be heroes, like your Robin Hood and his merry men, Liam. There will be books in the schools filled with pictures of our mischievous faces, with happy accounts of our adventures. Won't that be lovely, Nattrass? *Won't* it?"

"Yes," gasps Nattrass. *"Yes!"*

"Who were you fighting for?" I say.

"It was a mystery! They told us we were fighting for our government, that we were bringing order and freedom to our country and it was our duty to fight hard and well. When we whispered together, we children, we said that that was wrong. We said that we were rebels, in fact, that we were fighting for the people against an evil government, and that our cause was right. We said that God and the people were on our side. The truth is that we never knew. There was only war. There was no truth."

Nattrass struggles.

"What did I *tell* you, Nattrass? The knife will slip if you don't listen to me."

"Please, Oliver," I say.

He ignores me.

"The truth is," he whispers, "that I became a very good boy soldier. I took part in slaughter. I went into villages and rounded up children like me and showed them how to become like me. Can you imagine *that*, Nattrass? *Can* you?"

"Yes," gasps Nattrass. "Please let me go."

"No. Not yet. Now listen, brother. Now you must imagine a little more. You must imagine that you are me. Can you imagine that? *Can* you?"

"Yes. Anything. Get *off* me."

"Good. And imagine this: there is a village, an ordinary village like your village. Ordinary people living ordinary lives. It is an ordinary day. I think you cannot imagine Africa, so you must imagine it here. You must imagine your village, *your* people, *your* lives. Can you imagine that? *Can* you?"

"Yes," says Nattrass.

"Yes. But it is such a leap to the next thing you must imagine. But you *must* imagine. You have been walking all day through the fields of Northumberland with your troupe. You have been seeking this village. You have whisky and drugs inside you. You are carrying a knife, a gun. You are a soldier and you are nine years old. Can you imagine that? *Can* you?"

"No."

"No? But you *must*, brother. You have been nine years old, so you have memory to help you. And I am here beside you. I could not get closer to you, Nattrass. I am holding you so tight that we are almost one. I am whispering these things straight into your ear. And there is so much that I could whisper, but I ask you to imagine just one thing. So try. Will you try? *Will* you?"

"Yes."

"Good. So you are nine years old. You are me. And you have been ordered to take this village, Nattrass. Why? You do not know. The question 'Why?' does not matter. It is what soldiers do. Take villages, kill and burn. So you move into the village. There is much firing of guns, much screaming. Can you imagine? *Can* you?"

"No. Yes. I don't *know*."

"Suddenly . . . ," says Oliver.

He pauses. His hold on Nattrass seems to weaken, but Nattrass doesn't move.

"Suddenly," says Oliver, "there is a girl in front of you. She too must be nine years old. She is an ordinary girl, like your sister, perhaps, like any sister. Just like you were when you were nine years old, Nattrass. So you must be able to imagine that. There she is, before you, and she has a rock in her hand. And she is screaming, howling. She screams that her mother is gone, her father is gone. Imagine that, Nattrass. And now she is about to hit you with her rock. So what will you do? *What?*"

"I don't know."

"Then I will tell you, brother. And don't worry. You need not go on imagining. You are not me. I am Henry Meadows. I am the one who raises the knife. I am the one who screams and who plunges it deep into her heart."

Silence. Oliver loosens his grip. He steps back. He holds the knife out to Nattrass.

"Take it, Nattrass," he says. "Go on. Use it."

"You did that?" says Nattrass.

"Yes. I did. And it was just one of the many things I did. Take the knife. Go on. Imagine that knife in my heart. Imagine me dying at your feet. You'd be a hero, Nattrass. And I'd be gone."

Oliver steps closer to Nattrass. He holds out the knife.

"Do it!" he says.

The fire crackles, hisses. Crystal sobs. Suddenly, Death Dealer is sitting snugly at home in my hand. Nattrass takes a deep breath. He takes the knife. He raises his hand. I go for him.

"No!" yells Crystal.

"No!" yells Oliver.

Too late.

I rush at Nattrass. I knock him to the earth. I plunge the knife towards his heart.

And then there are more lights in the trees, and footsteps, and the soldiers have come for us.

now

1

It's hard to kill. And the knife was blunted by the rock. I knelt by Nattrass and saw his blood trickling to the earth. I saw my knife in his flesh. But I'd missed. The blade had gone into the flesh below his armpit. Hardly deep enough to hurt, never mind to kill.

The soldiers had been watching us all day, using us as imaginary renegades. They were young. They came through the trees. They stood around with their rifles resting in their arms. They smoked cigarettes, they shook their heads at us, they tut-tutted, they tried not to grin. They called for their doctor, who brought ointment and bandages.

Their captain was called Gareth Jones. He was in camouflage. His face was streaked with black. He glared at us. He took our knives away.

"We're not the law," he said. "It's not my job to find out who you are and where you're from and what the hell you think you're playing at. We could just leave you to it." He watched the doctor clean Nattrass's wound. "But what the hell *are* you playing at?"

He turned to me.

"You could have *killed* him," he said. "Did you *want* to kill him?"

"I'm sorry," I managed to gasp.

"I'm sorry," I gasped at Nattrass.

The captain spat.

"*Sorry?*" he said. "You're *sorry*? Do you not think there's enough death and destruction already in the world? Well?"

"Yes," I said.

He spat again.

"So what you playing at? And stop crying, will you?"

He sent for a truck. We climbed inside. He sat in the back with us and we were carried out of the valley and back towards the village.

"This is my fault," said Henry.

"And who might you be?" said Gareth Jones.

"I am Henry Meadows. I am from Liberia. I am a war criminal and a murderer."

The captain shook his head. He cursed.

"These are my friends," continued Oliver. "I have deceived them. It is me you must take away."

"Where we going?" said the captain.

I gave him my address. He phoned the police. He told them where to come to.

"You all right, son?" he said to Nattrass.

"Aye," said Nattrass.

"Good."

He glared at Crystal.

"And you?" he said. "What's your story?"

She shrugged.

"I ran away with Oliver. With Henry, I mean."

"With one or the other, eh?"

He thumped on the back of the driver's cab.

"Stop bouncing about, will you?" he yelled.

"Yes, Captain!" came a muffled reply.

The truck bounced on. The captain laid our knives out on his lap.

"You'd think we were in bloody Iraq!"

It was early morning. Dad was still up. He came to the door as the truck pulled up outside the house. He had a pen and notebook in his hand.

"There's been some trouble, Dad," I said.

The captain came up behind me.

"You're the father?" he said.

"Yes," said Dad. "What's going on?"

"Don't you think you should have known, sir?"

"Known what?"

The captain sighed. The others climbed out of the truck. The captain pointed to Nattrass's wound.

"The police are on their way," he said. "May we come in, sir?"

We streamed into the kitchen: Crystal, Henry Meadows, Gordon Nattrass, me, the captain. I heard Mum coming downstairs. She came to a halt in the kitchen doorway. She was in a dressing gown. Her hair was all tangled. Alison was in her arms.

"Oh, Mum," I whispered. My voice quavered and broke. "Look what I've done."

The baby giggled. She started jumping in Mum's arms.

"O-A!" she yelled as she pointed at me. "O-A! O-A!"

Monster. Monster.

2

Nattrass phoned his dad.

"Yes," he said. "Yes, the Lynches' house. Yes, I know what time it is. Yes, it's trouble." He sighed. I saw tears in his eyes. "Please, Dad. Please come for me." He put the phone down. "Him!" he muttered.

We sat at the table. Mum made tea and toast. Crystal held the baby. She cooed and smiled. Dad rested his chin on his hand.

"So?" he said.

I looked back into his eyes. He waited for the story, but where to start?

"We went to Kane's Cave," I said.

"Kane's Cave? Where's that?"

I looked down.

"I . . . I . . ."

I what? I dreamed of running away with Oliver and Crystal? I tried to kill a boy who used to be my friend? I was young? I was stupid?

I felt Crystal's hand on my arm.

"He tried to help us," she said. "That's all he did. To help us and protect us."

"O-A!" giggled Alison. "O-A!"

Dad found a map. He spread it out before us. He told me to show him. I pointed. Kane's Cave. I traced our route: the fields, the river, the moors, the hidden valley. We all leaned over it. Nattrass breathed the local names. Craw, St. Michael and All Angels, Rook Hall, the Tyne, the Roman Wall. He touched our little school, the field beside it. Crystal moved her hand beyond the map, traced the route back towards invisible Newcastle. Then Oliver: a sad sweep of his arm to show the great gulf of space and time towards his childhood in Liberia.

"It is me," said Oliver. "I must be taken away. Everything will be well again."

Then footsteps. And Mr. Nattrass was at the door. A hunched-over man, with the right arm of his coat pinned to the lapel.

"My boy," he said.

"He's here," said Dad.

Mr. Nattrass cast his eyes across us. I'd never seen him beyond his sofa-and-television room.

"So what's it this time?" he said.

"It's me, Mr. Nattrass," I said. "I . . . I attacked him with a knife."

He considered me for a moment. He grunted a little laugh.

194

"Did you now? Many a time I've wanted to do the same myself. What's the damage?"

Nattrass showed the dried blood on his clothes, showed the dressing. His father reached out and touched with his single hand.

"Hardly more than a scratch, eh?" He looked at me again. "A game that went wrong, was it?"

"No," I answered.

"He'll have asked for it, did he?"

"No," I answered.

"You sure? You're the one that used to come, aren't you, when both of you were little bairns?"

"Yes."

"I told him—they'll not want you if you go the way you're going. They'll have enough of you." He turned to his son. "Remember?"

Nattrass just stared emptily at him, seemed about to speak, then looked away, looked down.

"Never mind," said Mr. Nattrass. "You'll soon be free to go your own stupid way."

Then lights, and the police car, and Jenkins and Ball coming through the door.

"Well, well, *well*!" said Ball as he came in. "Now, why am I not surprised to see how *this* has all turned out?"

3

It seems so long ago, so far away, but it was here, at home, and just a few weeks back, when summer had begun to fade at last into the autumn. I tried to kill a boy and not much happened. Nattrass and his dad said it was a game that had gone wrong. We were boys, we were stupid, we didn't know what we were doing. I was a kid messing about with a pruning knife I thought was treasure. Nattrass was a country boy who whittled sticks, hunted rabbits, dreamed of living a country life from long ago. We were cautioned for carrying knives. Mr. Nattrass and my mum and dad were ordered to take more control of us.

"I knew," said PC Ball to me. "Soon as I saw you I thought, That one's headed for bother if nobody keeps a leash on him."

Oliver was taken away. He was not sent home to certain

death, of course. He is the worst of all victims, a child guided by monsters who were guided by monsters themselves. He is the child who has lost innocence, who has been taught to do evil. He is given our protection. And he is watched. And he is feared. Has the evil in him come to stay?

He comes to visit us. He comes with Crystal and their social workers. They are here today, this beautiful day in late October when the sky is bright and the air is cold, and our breath condenses around us, and leaves lie scattered on the grass.

He sits with Dad. He is writing his story again.

"This time," says Henry, "it will contain nothing but truth."

"If there is such a thing as truth," says Dad.

Henry contemplates for a time.

"Yes," he says. "There is truth, Mr. Lynch, and it must be told time and again and time and again and time and again. But sometimes the truth is found only after a journey through many lies."

Crystal plays with the baby. Their laughter rises, echoes. They crawl together over the fallen leaves. Crystal holds Alison's hands, and Alison awkwardly, joyously rises to her feet.

"Good girl!" says Crystal. "Oh what a good girl!"

Mum watches us all. She photographs us, but from a distance, making patterns of us against the sky, the grass, the trees, the ridges and the distant moors. She is happy. I know that she has begun to wonder about bringing Crystal or Henry or both of them into our family.

I wander alone in the garden. Ravens call from the fields.

There are always ravens. One day, I tell myself, the raven that began it all will flap down onto the grass before me. It will be followed by the hiker in the red hat. She will come into the garden and smile at Alison and tell us that Dad's tale is true. No, she could not care for her daughter. And yes, Alison's father was Thomas Fell, the man whose body was found in the north, the refugee from an ancient war.

So many mysteries, so many things to find out. I am growing, but I feel so young. I wander through the garden like a ghost. I go into the house. I find the money from the jar. I put it into a plastic bag. I go into Dad's study. Death Dealer is in there, lying beside the keyboard. I take the knife and return to the garden. I kneel, and I cut away a square of turf. I dig down, and find what I have always found—stones, roots, worms, dust. I clear a space. I put the money and the knife into the earth, then close it up again. I press the turf back into place. I watch the dust drying on my skin. The ravens call. The sun shines down. The baby cries out happily again. I look up from the earth and watch her totter to her feet again. I look at all of us, gathered here in this familiar garden, which has become so very strange.

david almond grew up in a large family in north-eastern England and says, "The place and the people have given me many of my stories." His first book for young people, *Skellig*, won the Carnegie Medal and the Whitbread Award, and was a Michael L. Printz Honor Book and an ALA-ALSC Notable Children's Book. *Skellig* has since become a hugely successful stage play, directed by Sir Trevor Nunn, an opera with music by Tod Machover, and a movie with Tim Roth in the title role. *Kit's Wilderness* won the Michael L. Printz Award for Excellence in Young Adult Literature. *The Fire-Eaters* won both the *Boston Globe–Horn Book* Award and the Whitbread Award. *Clay* became a TV movie on the BBC. David Almond's work has been translated into more than thirty languages, and he is widely acclaimed as one of the finest and most innovative children's writers in the world today. He lives with his family in Northumberland, surrounded by the landscapes of *Raven Summer*.